'You know t... love to you, ... feel the same...'

There was a pain around her heart and tears welled up in her eyes. In different circumstances she would have melted at his touch, told him joyously that she did feel the same, but how could she?

Unaware of the pain inside her, he tightened his arms and, holding her against the hard wall of his chest, he kissed her yearning mouth.

'Don't, Blair,' she begged.

'What is it?' he asked slowly. 'I thought...'

She took his hand and drew him to the sofa.

'I have something to tell you,' she said in a low voice. 'I'm pregnant.'

Abigail Gordon loves to write about the fascinating combination of medicine and romance from her home in a Cheshire village. She is active in local affairs and is even called upon to write the script for the annual village pantomime! Her eldest son is a hospital manager and helps with all her medical research. As part of a close-knit family, she treasures having two of her sons living close by and the third one not too far away. This also gives her the added pleasure of being able to watch her delightful grandchildren growing up.

Recent titles by the same author:

THE NURSE'S CHILD
FIRE RESCUE
PARAMEDIC PARTNERS
EMERGENCY RESCUE
THE NURSE'S CHALLENGE

THE PREGNANT POLICE SURGEON

BY
ABIGAIL GORDON

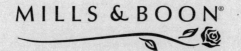

MILLS & BOON®

DID YOU PURCHASE THIS BOOK WITHOUT A COVER?

If you did, you should be aware it is **stolen property** as it was reported *unsold and destroyed* by a retailer. Neither the author nor the publisher has received any payment for this book.

All the characters in this book have no existence outside the imagination of the author, and have no relation whatsoever to anyone bearing the same name or names. They are not even distantly inspired by any individual known or unknown to the author, and all the incidents are pure invention.

All Rights Reserved including the right of reproduction in whole or in part in any form. This edition is published by arrangement with Harlequin Enterprises II B.V. The text of this publication or any part thereof may not be reproduced or transmitted in any form or by any means, electronic or mechanical, including photocopying, recording, storage in an information retrieval system, or otherwise, without the written permission of the publisher.

This book is sold subject to the condition that it shall not, by way of trade or otherwise, be lent, resold, hired out or otherwise circulated without the prior consent of the publisher in any form of binding or cover other than that in which it is published and without a similar condition including this condition being imposed on the subsequent purchaser.

MILLS & BOON and MILLS & BOON with the Rose Device are registered trademarks of the publisher.

First published in Great Britain 2003
Harlequin Mills & Boon Limited,
Eton House, 18-24 Paradise Road, Richmond, Surrey TW9 1SR

© Abigail Gordon 2003

ISBN 0 263 83451 4

Set in Times Roman 10½ on 12 pt.
03-0603-48200

Printed and bound in Spain
by Litografia Rosés, S.A., Barcelona

CHAPTER ONE

BLAIR NESBITT was met by a fresh spring dawn as he came out of the police station, and as he stepped into it there was a thoughtful expression on his face.

It had been a strange night. They usually were when he was called out by the forces of law and order to fulfil his role of police surgeon.

He sometimes wondered why he did it. There was enough trauma in the life of a GP without burdening himself with more, but for some reason he never considered opting out.

Maybe it was because of what had happened to his elder brother, Barney, all those years ago when he'd been slung into a police cell because they'd thought he'd been drunk and it had been a diabetic coma.

He had been drinking and the smell of it on his breath had made the constabulary think that alcohol had been the cause. The police surgeon who'd been sent for had been zealous and very thorough and had probably saved his life by his expertise and quick thinking.

It had been a long time ago and now, with the diabetes strictly under control, his brother was happily married with two teenage girls. Barney had probably forgotten the incident, but he hadn't.

Every time he was called out to someone in the cells he was acutely aware that, no matter what they'd done, incarcerated behind that locked door they were at risk if anything went wrong with their physical well-being.

Tonight had been one of those peculiar nights when the circumstances that had brought him to the city's largest police station had been odd to say the least.

He'd been called out because a domestic dispute had resulted in an enraged ex-husband being arrested on an assault charge against his ex-wife's new partner, and no sooner had the man been put into a cell than he'd started having convulsions.

By the time that Blair had got there he'd been told by the desk sergeant that the man had come out of the fit and that they'd troubled him unnecessarily.

'Why would that be?' he asked, having no intention of accepting that as a reason for not seeing the patient.

The desk sergeant was showing signs of embarrassment as he explained, 'After I'd sent for you, Dr Nesbitt, we had a breakdown in communications. I was called away and one of the other officers, thinking that I hadn't been in touch, called your place. Obviously you weren't there as you were already on your way here. So he got in touch with someone else on the police surgeon rota and she's in there with him now.'

He would settle for that, he thought. Just as long as there was a doctor at the scene. But it was a pity they'd got him out of bed for nothing.

'Who did he send for?' he asked casually. 'I don't recall any women on the list.'

The sergeant consulted paperwork in front of him and said, 'Dr Rossiter. Imogen Rossiter.'

'And who might she be, I wonder?' he said in some surprise. 'New on the list and a woman! That makes a refreshing change.'

Footsteps had been approaching from the rear. They weren't the heavy pacing of policeman's feet and the voice that went with them was sweeter and more melodious than those of any of the sergeant's colleagues.

But it was cool, too, as the woman who was now facing them said, 'You sound surprised to find a woman GP here at this hour, although it's obviously nothing new for you to be here. Might I ask who you are?'

She was small, curvy, raven-haired, with bright hazel eyes in a face that was one of the most captivating he'd ever seen. His surprise at meeting her under such circumstances was increasing by the minute.

His smile when it flashed out had been known to make susceptible members of the opposite sex go weak at the knees, but it seemed that was not to be the case with Dr Imogen Rossiter.

'I'm Blair Nesbitt,' he said easily. 'GP and police surgeon when I am needed.'

'So where were you tonight when you were needed?' the captivating one asked in the same cool tone.

'Where I usually am at that time of night. Asleep in my bed…and the moment I was called out I set off for this place. But the sergeant here and his staff got things a bit mixed up. You were called out, too, and as you beat me to it you obviously live nearer than I do.'

He quirked a quizzical eyebrow. 'Does that answer your question?'

'Er…yes. I suppose so.'

'And now I've got a question for you.'

'What is it?'

'Are you by any chance related to Brian Rossiter, the chief constable?'

'He's my father.'

The sergeant was observing her with respectful surprise as he exclaimed, 'You never said!'

She shrugged.

'Why should I? I'm not my father's keeper, nor is he mine. I'm in medicine and he's in law and order.'

'You *are* involved in what your father does up to a point, though,' Blair said in the same easy tone, pointing in the direction of the cells, 'or you wouldn't be doing this job.'

'I'm doing it to keep the wolf from the door while I look round for a practice to join,' she informed him.

'Really? So you are a qualified GP?'

'Yes, I am. Does that surprise you?'

'No, not at all,' he said smoothly. 'Except…'

Tossing her dark mop, she eyed him levelly. 'Except that I don't look old enough, you were about to say?'

Blair found himself smiling. This one was something else. The interesting face went with a riveting personality if the way she was pinning him down was anything to go by.

'Yes. I was, as a matter of fact, but obviously I was wrong.'

'Everybody thinks that. Even my father, who is well aware of my age, thinks I'm too young.'

'What for exactly?'

'Oh, a lot of things. One of them being that he thinks I should still be living at home instead of doing my own thing.'

'I do hope that this prolonged conversation means that the man in the cells is out of danger,' he said equably. 'I'd hate to think that while we are chatting he was having another fit or something.'

'Of course he's all right,' she said swiftly. 'I wouldn't have left him otherwise. The poor guy had suffered a grand mal seizure and when he came round he was sleepy and disorientated, but not so much that

I didn't get the idea that he was more sinned against than sinning on the domestic scene.

'He's in a natural sleep now and should wake up none the worse. He was on the bed in the cell when he had the fit, so didn't injure himself in any way. If you do have any more problems, either send for me again or have him admitted to hospital,' she told the sergeant, 'but at the moment he's all right. Apparently he's had epilepsy for some time and due to the upset hadn't taken his medication.'

Turning back to Blair, Imogen said, 'I'll say good-night, Dr Nesbitt. If you hear of any vacancies for GPs in local practices I'd be obliged if you'd let me know.' And with a swing of slender hips inside a bright red skirt that was topped by a navy blazer she picked up her bag and prepared to leave.

Blair was about to do the same when the phone on the desk rang. As the sergeant listened to what was being said at the other end he motioned for them to stay.

'There's been an accident upstairs in the staff canteen,' he said. 'Pan of hot fat dropped and two people with burns. Can one of you take a look at them as you're already on the premises?'

The two doctors eyed each other and Blair said, 'I'll deal with it if you like, so that you can get off home.'

'I'm in no rush. I'll come with you,' she said.

The woman who'd been carrying the pan of oil had spilt it over her legs and feet and another canteen assistant who'd been passing at the time had received splashes on the arms.

The most badly burnt of the two was crying out with pain when they arrived in the dining area of the police station and they were told that an ambulance had been sent for.

Imogen fell to her knees beside the injured woman and held her hand, while Blair reached into his case for non-stick dressings to cover the affected areas until the emergency services arrived.

The faces of the two doctors were grave as they observed the extent of the burns. The woman was in a state of shock, with lowered blood pressure and a rapid pulse. The other casualty was sitting white-faced and speechless with a tea-towel wrapped around her arm.

Feet pounding up the stairs announced the arrival of the paramedics and as the two doctors handed the women into their care Imogen said, 'We'd better watch that we don't slip on any of the grease that's all over the place, or one of us could be the next one bound for A and E.'

At that moment, almost as if she'd wished it upon herself, her feet shot from under her and it was only Blair's arms reaching out for her that kept her upright.

As he looked down into a pair of wary hazel eyes he wanted to laugh. What did she think he was going to do? Turn what could have been a mishap into a provocative moment?

It was five o'clock in the morning and the last thing on his mind was making something out of such a happening. Yet he had to admit that he was enjoying holding her close for a short time. In the stale confines of the police station she smelt fresh and clean.

One of the canteen staff was hovering, ready to tackle the grease with a bucket and mop, and, still with his hand on her arm, he said, 'Let's go, shall we? I have a surgery at half past eight and I wouldn't mind a couple of hours' sleep first.'

Imogen nodded.

'Me, too, with regard to the sleep, but as I'm still here I might as well check on the epileptic guy again before I leave.' She held out a small capable hand. 'So, bye for now…until we meet again.'

As he took her hand in his, Blair smiled.

'I'll shake on that…Dr Rossiter.' And off he went into the breaking dawn.

As she drove back to the apartment in the city centre that was her pride and joy, Imogen was grimacing. The last thing she'd expected when she'd been called out had been meeting another police surgeon attending the same patient.

Blair Nesbitt had seemed a bit wary of her at first, which had prompted her to come over all cocky, and now she was regretting it. As she was regretting having admitted kinship to the new chief constable.

She could have prevaricated without telling an ab-solute lie, but instead, as usual, she'd gone rushing in head first and had admitted that she was related to the head of the county's police force.

Obviously being Brian Rossiter's daughter wasn't anything to be ashamed of, but it wasn't anything she went around boasting about either. She valued her in-dependence and had acquired the appointment as police surgeon on her own merits, hence the desk sergeant's surprise when he'd discovered who she was.

Her mother had died some years previously and her father had recently remarried. A happening that she'd been totally in favour of as for one thing it gave him less time to try to run her life, and for another she liked Celia, his new wife, and thought she would be good for him.

Before she'd gone to work in the Midlands as a trainee GP Imogen had lived with him in the big house that went with his status in the county, but the moment he'd introduced Celia into his life she herself had been off to pastures new and when she'd returned she'd found herself an apartment in the city centre, almost on top of the police station. It was a haven filled with bright, modern furnishings and her favourite things from childhood.

Where did he live? she wondered. She'd heard a powerful car drive off as she'd been coming from the cells but hadn't had the chance to see what it looked like or in which direction it had been heading.

'Bye for now,' she'd said to him as he was leaving and had followed it up with a trite, 'until we meet again,' which must have made him think that she wanted to get to know him better.

That was not the case at all. She'd recently had her fill of liaisons with attractive members of the opposite sex. Though, come to think of it, Sean Derwent hadn't been in the same class as the Nesbitt guy, but he'd been presentable enough for her to think she'd been in love with him.

However, sadly Sean was in the past. In every way but one, she told herself sombrely. She'd begged him not to go mountaineering on such dangerous terrain but he'd just laughed and gone anyway.

Her worst fears had been realised with the news that the young geologist and his friend, Tom, had perished in bad weather conditions on Everest.

After coping with the devastation of such sudden loss, she had been struggling to get on with life without him, but she wasn't being very successful and for a very good reason. She was pregnant.

She'd only slept with Sean once and they had taken precautions, but a faulty contraceptive had let them down and now here she was, having to face up to the fact that he wasn't going to be around any more and she had the sole responsibility of the precious child that she was carrying.

Even before he'd died she'd begun to accept that Sean wasn't going to be the love of her life. He had been good fun, attractive, but there had always been an inclination there to put himself first and she had often wondered since how he would have coped with the thought of fatherhood.

As for herself, after the first shock of finding that she was pregnant had subsided, she'd felt scared, excited and very protective of the child she was carrying inside her.

But it hadn't stopped her from feeling trapped, too. She adored children, had always longed for the brothers and sisters that her parents had never given her, but now that she was to have a child of her own there was the responsibility of it that was going to weigh her down if she wasn't careful.

At the present time she was just over two and a half months pregnant. Soon her condition would become evident. Her father would find out and as she was already a source of irritation to him, it would only add fuel to the fire.

In the meantime, she needed to find herself a niche in a local practice because the role of a penniless single mother did not appeal to her and it would appeal even less to the man who was in charge of the county's constabulary.

He'd worked his way through the ranks and was quick to remind anyone who might overlook the fact.

Respectability was Brian Rossiter's lifeblood. She'd often thought it was because he'd seen so much of what was not 'respectable' in his career that it meant so much to him.

To find his only daughter in circumstances that didn't meet his standards would bring about a situation that she didn't yet want to contemplate. Though she would soon have no choice as her waistline thickened.

The man she'd just met must be based somewhere not too far away if he was on call to the police station, she thought, channelling her thinking processes back to the night that was past. What sort of a set-up was he involved in? she wondered. Group practice? Solo concern? There weren't many of those these days.

He'd been quite something. Straight as a ramrod. Broad-shouldered, slim-hipped, with a thick fair thatch above eyes of darkest brown in a lived-in sort of face.

Had he gone home to some young Nesbitts and a sleeping wife? Imogen sighed. It shouldn't matter to her if he'd returned to his own personal harem! It was what was going on in her own life that she had to be concerned about, and it was all about responsibilities and reality.

Weariness was upon her now, like an indefinable cloak, and as she put her key in the lock for once she was glad that an empty day loomed ahead.

As Blair climbed the stairs to resume his broken sleep the closed door of Simon's room was an indication that his young brother was at home and in bed. He smiled. He wasn't the only one whose occupation took him into the city in the small hours of the night.

Simon was employed as a chef in a late night restaurant and was rarely home before four a.m. He made up for it with a prolonged lie-in in the mornings, but it didn't stop Blair from wishing that the twenty-two-year-old worked more sociable hours, both for his health's sake and his safety.

There were three of them—Barney, who lived with his family in Herefordshire, himself in the middle and then Simon, conceived rather late in his mother's life.

And now, with both their parents dead, he had his younger brother living with him until such time that he could afford a place of his own.

Simon was untidy and irresponsible about everything but his job, which he adored, and Blair forgave him most things because of that.

At thirty-five, he never seemed to have the time to do anything about his own unmarried state. As senior partner in a thriving group practice, he was kept well occupied and then there was his function as police surgeon to fulfil. Yet he was aware that if the right person came along he would make time.

There'd been Andrea of course. The manipulator. Sweet, clinging and dangerous. When he'd resisted the advances of the trainee GP who'd come to them for experience, and had made it very clear that he hadn't been interested in her, she'd tried to ruin his reputation by spreading rumours of malpractice, but it hadn't worked. Blair had been known for his integrity and he'd sent her packing.

The aftermath of the Andrea affair had been that ever since then when he'd taken a woman GP into the practice, either trained or in training, he'd been wary.

There would be a vacancy coming up in two weeks' time. One of the partners was moving south to be near his wife's relatives.

Blair had only found out a couple of days ago and

hadn't been over-pleased at such short notice, but as there was sudden illness involved on the part of the man's in-laws he'd had to accept the inevitable with good grace.

Interviews would be taking place in the next few days and as he climbed thankfully into bed the vision of bright hazel eyes and a very kissable mouth came to mind. What was it that Imogen Rossiter had said? If he heard of any vacancies in local practices she would be obliged if he would let her know.

He couldn't see himself doing that. Not with regard to his own practice anyway. From what he'd seen of her on short acquaintance, the captivating daughter of the chief constable would make the departed Andrea seem positively meek.

Yet with all that bounce and style he didn't visualise Imogen developing a fixation for him. She would be looking out for younger fish to fry.

In spite of the fact that she'd been quick to point out that she was trained and ready to take up work in a local practice, he'd like to bet that it was only recently that she'd been able to say that. If she was a day over twenty-seven he would be surprised.

As he closed his eyes for a quick catnap before morning surgery he thought drowsily that the pedantic chief constable seemed an unlikely parent for her.

Brian Rossiter was one of his patients and on the few occasions that their paths had crossed he'd struck him as being a rather boring control freak. Which was probably the reason for his daughter's lack of enthusiasm when he'd asked her if they were related.

Where had *she* been, though? He hadn't even known that the fellow had a daughter. But if she didn't fit into the mould he'd made for her he supposed that Rossiter wouldn't be advertising the fact.

It almost made him feel like asking her to come along to be interviewed for the vacancy at his practice. But before he could make a decision on that, sleep had claimed him.

The idea was still there as Blair took morning surgery and he told himself that was the only reason he was considering it…because Brian Rossiter was a pain. It wasn't because for the first time in years he was attracted to a woman. No. It definitely wasn't that.

He rang Imogen at midday after looking her number up in the phone book and was answered by a sleepy voice that had none of the nocturnal vibrance that had so entranced him.

'It's Blair Nesbitt here,' he announced crisply.

'Who?' she asked on a yawn.

'Blair Nesbitt, Imogen. We met only hours ago. Surely you haven't forgotten.'

There was silence for a moment and he visualised her pulling herself up on the pillows and raking a hand through her dark mop.

'No. Of course I haven't forgotten,' she said in slow surprise. 'You don't let the grass grow under your feet, do you?'

'And what is that supposed to mean?' he asked with raised brows.

'That you want to see me again. That's what usually happens between the sexes, isn't it?' she asked flippantly.

'Huh! I'm afraid that you're presuming too much,' he replied, trying not to laugh. 'I'm ringing to say there's a vacancy coming up in the practice where I'm senior partner and I'm interviewing in the near future if you're interested.'

'Oops!' she said unrepentantly. 'Serves me right for jumping in before I'd heard the full story. I don't suppose that I've improved my chances.'

'No, you haven't,' he agreed blandly, 'and don't think that because you're related to the top brass it will make any difference as far as I'm concerned.'

He had a feeling that would get to her, and it did.

'If you think I would try using my father's name to get on in the world, you are very much mistaken,' she hit back frostily.

'Good. So now we understand each other. Getting back to the reason for my call, do you want to be considered for the post?'

'Yes,' she breathed. 'Of course I do. Give me a place and a time and I'll be there.'

'Tomorrow at one-fifteen at the Sycamores practice.'

'That's strange. I went to school with one of the receptionists there and I asked her a couple of weeks ago if there were any vacancies, but she said no.'

'That would have been so at the time, but one of my partners is having to move in a hurry and we're going to be doing some reshuffling. And now I have to go as I've got a list of house calls here in front of me. So I'll see you tomorrow then.'

'Yes, Dr Nesbitt,' she said meekly.

'There's no need to be servile because of your mistaken presumptions,' he told her with the urge to laugh coming over him again. Hoping that he'd taken the wind out of her sails for a second time, he rang off.

And if that wasn't the craziest thing he'd done in a long time he didn't know what was, Blair thought as he set off on his rounds.

*   *   *

If Imogen had been half-asleep before, she wasn't now. Her mind was in overdrive. Would Blair take her on? And if he did offer her the position, did she want it?

Every moment of their meeting the night before was clear in her mind. She'd felt instinctively that he was interesting and different from other men she'd met.

He had a craggy sort of face and a manner that said he would stand no messing around. And with that thought in mind she began to debate what would happen if he offered her the position and then had to be told she was pregnant.

She'd always told herself that if this ever happened to her...an unwanted pregnancy...she would have a termination. Yet the moment she'd made the mind-blowing discovery she had known that there was no way she could even contemplate it.

So, with this other thing that was happening in her life at the moment, Blair would have to know if there was any chance of her becoming part of the Sycamores Practice.

As she tried to ignore the nausea that was becoming a regular part of each morning, Imogen eyed herself in the mirror.

Don't cross your bridges before you get to them, she told the white face staring back at her. Blair might already be having second thoughts after the boob you made. And how will you feel if he is? Mildly disappointed? Philosophical? Or, more like it, mortified because you want to get to know him better?

When Blair told his two partners that they would be interviewing the chief constable's daughter as a possible addition to the practice, there were expressions of surprise.

'And so where did you meet Imogen Rossiter?' Andrew Travis, an elderly widower and golfing fanatic, asked with a smile. 'I didn't know she was back in these parts.'

Bill Robertson, who was about to take himself and his young family off to the southern counties, nodded his approval and commented that a lot of the women patients preferred having their own sex to treat them and that it was some time since they'd had a woman doctor in the practice.

'Yes, well, we'll have to see how she comes across during the interview,' Blair said casually, with the memory of a challenging hazel gaze in an unforgettable face in mind. 'You might not think her suitable.'

'Your opinion is more important than ours,' Andrew pointed out. 'I'll be retiring soon and Bill here is going anyway, so it will be a case of who you want to help run the practice, Blair.'

With that the subject was dropped—to be revived the next day when the three of them gathered in his consulting room to await the arrival of the interviewee.

When Imogen was shown into the room by one of the receptionists Blair's eyes widened. This was not the dazzler of two nights ago. She looked pale and subdued and he immediately thought that maybe she'd been on some sort of high on that other occasion and this was the real Imogen Rossiter. If that was the case, there would be none more disappointed than he.

She perked up during the interview but the sparkle was still missing. Yet it was Imogen Rossiter's qualifications they were concerned with, not her charm, or lack of it, he told himself. There was nothing wrong with her track record. She'd studied medicine at a London college, had got a first-class honours degree and had done her GP training with a practice in the Midlands.

He'd known she would be good. It had been there in her manner, and if today's less buoyant approach was disconcerting, what did it matter?

Blair wasn't to know that Imogen had spent the last twenty-four hours wrestling with her conscience, trying to decide if she should tell the three doctors that she was pregnant, though she knew she wasn't obliged to. They would know soon enough anyway, she'd kept telling herself. More to the point, she needed to be positive in her own mind that she could carry this job through her pregnancy. She had to, she needed to.

She'd never slept around until that night spent with Sean, and had never dreamt that a pregnancy would be the result. She would have liked to have been able to make the choice between marriage and single parent-hood, but it hadn't worked out that way.

Now he was gone and the knowledge that the tiny foetus inside her was going to be fatherless wasn't easy to come to terms with. But, she kept telling herself, she would have enough love for both of them. Her baby wasn't going to suffer because of the circumstances of its conception.

In the end she'd decided that she would let the in-terview take its course. There would be time enough to tell Blair later if she got the job.

The moment they'd had eye contact again Imogen had known how much she wanted to be part of the practice, and that had been something else to take away her usual poise.

Blair was getting to his feet and holding out his

hand. His grip was firm and, she hoped, reassuring. Yet he was saying with a smooth sort of finality that did nothing to raise her hopes, 'I'll be in touch during the next few days. We still have a couple of people to interview.'

She flashed him a tentative smile and again he wondered what had happened to the woman he'd met in the police station, as the one standing in front of him, murmuring her polite goodbyes, was nothing like her.

As she drove home Imogen was coming out of the stupor that had overtaken her during the interview. What on earth had possessed her to be so negative, she thought furiously, when she was nothing like that normally?

If it was her condition, it would have been better to come clean there and then as she wasn't going to be of much use in a busy practice in that sort of state.

Yet she knew that it was more mental than physical. She'd felt during the interview that she was being swept along by a strong current, that her hopes and aspirations had been taken out of her control. She would be devastated if she didn't get the job. Because without it there would be no Blair Nesbitt in her life.

CHAPTER TWO

'AND so did you not want to stay with the practice in Birmingham where you'd trained?' Blair had asked at one stage of the interview.

'No,' Imogen had told him. 'I wanted to come back to Manchester. It's the area I know best. My roots are here.'

It was only partly true. She'd wanted to leave Birmingham because that was where she'd met Sean. There were too many upsetting memories connected with the place. But she wasn't going to tell him that. Not at this stage of their acquaintance anyway.

And now all she had to do was wait until she heard from him, and if it was a thumbs-down then she would have to look elsewhere.

When she got back to the apartment there was a message from Celia on the answering-machine to ask if she would like to dine with the newly-weds that evening.

'Your dad says we've hardly seen anything of you since the wedding,' she said when Imogen rang back, 'and you know he does miss you.'

'Only because he likes to boss me around,' she replied.

Her new stepmother laughed.

'It's the job that makes him like that. You know what the police force is like. Yes, sir! No, sir! So you'll come, then,' she wheedled.

'Yes, of course,' Imogen agreed. 'If only to see you.'

She was thinking that this visit would be a good idea as the pregnancy wasn't showing yet. Afterwards she could leave it for a few months before she saw them again and by then her father would have no choice but to accept the situation.

One thing that might make it easier for him to adjust to the idea of her becoming a single parent was the fact that the baby's father was dead. There would be no need for him to go rampaging off to Birmingham to insist that Sean do the honourable thing.

Strangely, at this moment she was more concerned with what Blair would think about her circumstances than what her father would have to say.

'And so what have you been up to lately?' her father asked in his best interrogatory tone as they faced each other across the dining table.

'Not a lot,' she told him smoothly.

'Have you found yourself a job?'

'I'm hoping to be taken on at a local practice. I went for an interview this morning…and I've been put on the police surgeon rota.'

'I see. No one has informed me of that fact.'

Imogen laughed. 'Well, they wouldn't, would they? Surely such minor matters aren't brought to your attention.'

He was observing her beneath bushy brows with piercing blue eyes that were softer when he looked at Celia, but were still judgmental with everyone else.

'Not when it concerns my daughter.'

'Yes, well, that wasn't mentioned,' she responded airily, and saw Celia hide a smile.

He ignored the comment and went on to ask, 'And

which practice is it that you have been interviewed for?'

'The Sycamores.'

'Really! I'm a patient there. I changed doctors recently. Blair Nesbitt is my GP.'

Imogen's spirits sank to zero and then bounced
quickly back. The last thing she'd expected if she was
taken on by Blair was to be coming across her father
during surgery hours.

It wasn't the done thing for a doctor to treat a family
member so she wouldn't have that prospect facing her.
Either Blair or Andrew Travis would see him if he
should require a consultation, and in any case her father
would rather take his ailments to the local greengrocer
than have to discuss them with his difficult daughter.

Celia was tuned in to both their minds and, putting
an affectionate arm around the straight-backed figure
beside her, she said with a smile, 'Then if Imogen joins
the Sycamores practice it will be a double bonus whenever you need to seek medical advice, darling. The ad-
mirable Dr Nesbitt will be there to advise you on your
health and you'll be able to have a nice chat with your
daughter if she isn't too busy.'

He smiled back at her with real affection and Imogen
thought without rancour that it was good to know that
someone could get through to the old tartar.

She was too much like her mother for them to ever
be compatible. A free spirit who wasn't chained to respectability was how he saw her, and when he discovered that she was carrying a child, that opinion wasn't
likely to change.

When the buzzer sounded at Imogen's apartment a couple of days later, she was in the bathroom, retching.

It was eight o'clock in the morning, she thought weakly. Who on earth would be calling at this time? When she checked the intercom audio-visual system her jaw dropped in dismay. Blair Nesbitt was standing outside the apartment, checking the time on his watch and tapping his foot impatiently.

After she'd told him to come up and had released the locks on her door, she forced back the nausea and hurried into the bathroom.

She knew that she looked a sight without checking in the mirror. The moment she'd opened her eyes she'd felt queasy, and without even putting a brush through her hair, had gone into the bathroom in the same naked state in which she'd slept.

There was a white towelling robe hung up behind the door and, grabbing it, she flung it on and reached for a hairbrush, but the doorbell was already ringing. Blair was outside on the doormat.

'Good grief!' he exclaimed without preamble when she opened her front door. 'Where were you last night? Clubbing?'

'I suppose that means I'm not the choicest sight you've seen this morning.'

'Correct. You'll have to be up and about earlier than this when you're taking morning surgery.'

She'd been about to straighten out her tangled mop but the comment had brought her to a standstill and now, with the brush suspended above her scalp, she was observing him with widening eyes.

'Are you speaking in general terms?' she asked. 'Or are you the bearer of glad tidings?'

'I don't know about it being glad tidings,' he said drily, 'but, yes, the position is yours, if you want it.'

She was perking up by the moment, her rumpled appearance forgotten.

'Of course I want to come and work at the Sycamores,' she said laughingly. 'There is just one fly in the ointment, though. I discovered last night that my father is a patient at the practice and we don't exactly see eye to eye.'

'What is it with the two of you?' he questioned.

She shrugged slim shoulders inside the bulky robe. 'Conflict of personalities.'

'Yes, well, as long as there's none of that with regard to the practice, what you do in your own time is nothing to do with me. And the chief constable is my patient anyway. You won't be involved and in any case he only consults me rarely.'

While he'd been putting that problem into perspective, Imogen's mind had been on the much bigger one that as yet he didn't know about. She'd been avoiding the truth when she'd said there was only one fly in the ointment. There were two, and now was an ideal moment to mention the other one. But the words wouldn't come out and with a queasy feeling in her stomach that wasn't connected with the morning sickness she knew that she was going to let the moment pass. There would be plenty of time to tell him about her pregnancy.

'So we have an agreement?' he was asking.

'Yes.'

'Right. I'll get the practice manager to put it in writing. When can you start? The sooner the better so that you can get settled in before Bill leaves for pastures new.'

'Er…tomorrow?'

Blair nodded.

'Why not? Once you're in place we'll have to discuss how we're going to fit in our police surgeon commitments so that they don't clash.'

'Yes, of course,' she murmured, her mind awash with what it was all going to mean.

'That's where I've been this morning,' Blair said as he turned to go. 'On police surgeon business.'

She was fully tuned in now.

'In what way?'

'Road rage incident on the motorway in the early morning rush hour. The two men concerned started fighting and ended up in the police cells. Apparently they both seemed all right when they were arrested but one of them complained of head pains from when he'd hit the ground during the scuffle and so they called me out to check him over.

'There weren't any visible signs of damage to the skull. His vision was OK, so was his co-ordination, but I recommended that he be taken to Casualty to have an X-ray. I don't taken any chances that someone locked up on my patch might come to grief in the cells through lack of medical care.'

'Well, of course,' she agreed slowly, 'but you say that as if there's a special reason why you feel that way.'

'There is. Many years ago my elder brother was locked up mistakenly. They thought he was in a drunken stupor when it was a diabetic coma. If it hadn't been for the efficient police surgeon who was called out to him he could have died.'

'So you have a brother? Any more family besides him?'

'Yes, there are three of us. One brother older, one younger. Simon, the youngest, is living with me until such time as he can afford a place of his own. Our parents died some years ago and I've looked out for him ever since.'

'You aren't married, then?'

He shook his head.

'Never found the time or the right woman, and have felt even less inclined to get involved with anyone since I had an unpleasant experience with a young GP some time ago. I found her deceitful and conniving.'

Dismay was swamping her. Deceitful…conniving… What was he going to think she was in the very near future?

'And yet you're taking me on?'

He laughed.

'Yes. Lightning doesn't usually strike twice. I'm willing to take the risk.'

If Imogen hadn't been feeling so demoralised to hear about her disruptive predecessor she would have bounced back and told him that she wasn't asking for favours. But his description of the other woman was like a death knell to her hopes.

'I really do have to go,' Blair said, breaking into the silence that had fallen. 'Morning surgery starts at half past eight. So we'll see you tomorrow.' With a quizzical lift of one eyebrow he added, 'Have you got an alarm clock?'

'Yes. Why? You surely don't think I'll oversleep on my first day?' she flashed back indignantly.

'Maybe not, but from where I'm standing…'

'Don't judge a book by its cover, Dr Nesbitt. For your information, I was in bed by ten o'clock last night. On my own and completely sober.'

He was frowning.

'So why…? You're not ill, are you?'

'No. I'm not ill. I'm in glowing health.'

He was eyeing her doubtfully and she thought that the last thing she should be doing was directing his attention to her physical state.

When he'd gone she went to the window and watched him walk across the forecourt of the apartments to where he'd parked his car. He had style and authority, his life all mapped out, knew exactly where he was going, while she was in chaos.

She'd found somewhere that she wanted to work and someone that she wanted to get to know better, but she was going about it all in the wrong way, she thought dismally. Would Blair Nesbitt think that history was repeating itself when he discovered her secret?

Lauren Brown, the receptionist she'd been at school with, observed her in pleased surprise when Imogen strolled into the practice the next day.

She'd got her poise back this morning, was thinking positively and about to make a statement about her capabilities. Just as long as the nausea she'd experienced earlier didn't return. If it did she would have to conceal it in the best way she could.

'Blair said we were to have a new doctor starting this morning.' Lauren said after they'd given each other a hug, 'but I didn't expect it to be you after I'd told you there were no vacancies.'

'I looked for you when I came for the interview,' Imogen told her, 'but someone said it was your day off. Dr Nesbitt and I met at the police station after we'd both been called out to the same person and I asked him to let me know if he heard of any vacancies. Lo and behold, he came back to me on it. And here I am.'

'If you'd like to step into the office my partners are

waiting, and once we've given you a briefing the day can get under way,' Blair's voice said from behind her.

She swivelled round and when she saw his expression Imogen felt that, whatever the future held, at this moment he was observing her favourably.

She was immaculate in a black tailored suit and white silk blouse, offset with sheer tights and black leather shoes with a sensible heel. Her hair was brushed into a smooth cap and her make-up as light and flattering as her perfume.

She saw amusement in his eyes and knew why. He guessed that this was to wipe out her unimpressive appearance of the previous morning. His next comment was proof of it.

'So you did manage to get up in time,' he remarked in a low voice. 'The effect is worthy of the effort.'

'I'm so glad you approve,' she told him smoothly. 'Yesterday you caught me at an awkward moment.'

'Well, you certainly looked ghastly,' he remarked, adding with his brow creasing into a frown, 'I know I asked you this yesterday, but I feel I must ask again. You aren't ill, are you?'

Imogen shook her head.

'I assure you that I'm not suffering from anything that might affect my work here.'

Taking her arm, he propelled her towards the door of the office.

The other two partners were affable enough, yet not all that keyed into the prospect of another doctor on the team, but as one of them was leaving in a few days' time and the other looked to be nearing retirement age, she supposed it wasn't surprising.

And the advantage of that situation was that it would throw Blair and herself together more once the others had gone. Just as long as he wasn't going to feel that in her case lightning *had* struck twice.

To counteract that possibility she needed to make herself indispensable so, taking off her jacket, she straightened the cuffs of her blouse and asked coolly. 'Which room is mine?'

'The small one next to mine,' Blair told her. 'There is a connecting door, so if you have any problems don't hesitate to bring them to me. And, Imogen, welcome to the Sycamores.'

Her smile flashed out and in the bright hazel gaze that met his was a promise of good things to come. At least he hoped that was what he was seeing there.

When he'd called at her apartment the previous day Blair had known that he'd been acting out of character. For one thing, it wasn't the done thing to call on someone who was a comparative stranger at that hour. And for another, there had been no need to go personally to tell Imogen that the vacancy was hers if she wanted it. He could have phoned just as easily.

But he'd wanted to see her again. To be in her presence. He'd met her twice previously and on both occasions she'd been a different person—the first time confident and bouncy, and the second much more subdued. He hoped that she wasn't going to be so unpredictable now she was working with him.

Imogen's first patient was a young mother who'd found a lump in her breast. On examining her, she confirmed that there was indeed a lump there. It was small but an alien swelling nevertheless.

'I'm going to send you for a biopsy,' Imogen told her. 'It's possible that it's benign but we can't take any chances. Is there any history of breast cancer in the family?'

The patient nodded glumly.

'Yes. My mum's had it in the past and my sister's got it now. I've been waiting for this to happen.'

Imogen observed her sympathetically. What an awful prospect for this poor woman to have hanging over her. It was obviously in the genes. But that didn't mean that this was another case of cancer. Life wasn't always that predictable.

'And did your mother recover?'

'Yes.'

She took the woman's clenched hand in hers and said gently, 'Let's keep an open mind, shall we, until the results come through? I know this is a very anxious time for you, but if your mother overcame the illness that does provide some reassurance if the test should prove positive.'

'Yes, I suppose so,' the patient agreed with the vestige of a smile. 'But it doesn't take away the dread of being the next victim of a family curse.'

Imogen nodded. There wasn't a lot she could say to that. Inherited illnesses were the nightmares that some families had to live with.

When she'd gone, the communicating door between the two rooms opened and Blair said, 'So? How did it go with your first patient?'

'Fine,' she told him with the gravity of what she had just been hearing still upon her. 'A lump in the breast.'

Blair nodded.

'Yes, she asked to see a woman doctor so it was fortunate, you being here.'

'It must have sometimes been inconvenient when you were an all-male team,' she remarked.

He smiled.

'Yes, it was, so we are very pleased to have you here. By the way, while we have a moment to spare, how did you get on the police surgeons' register, if it wasn't by pulling strings?'

Imogen eyed him mutinously.

'If you mean did I tell the authorities who I was, no, I didn't. I don't want to rise in the profession by climbing on my father's shoulders. I'd done some police surgeon work in Birmingham that had been described as very satisfactory, so there was no problem. I feel the same as you, that those in the cells should receive the same care as those who consult us here.'

As the morning progressed Imogen found she was enjoying herself. Since leaving Birmingham, she'd missed the atmosphere of the practice and the varied number of ailments that each day brought.

One of her patients was a seventeen-year-old girl, very tall, easily six feet, who said with quiet determination that she wanted to be made smaller.

Her mother was with her and the woman was totally fraught at the prospect of what her daughter was asking for.

After the first few moments of surprise Imogen talked to the girl gently, aware of the presence of strong undercurrents.

'You *are* tall,' she agreed, 'but so are most young people these days. It's folk like myself who are in the minority.'

'Men don't like tall women,' she was told gloomily.

Nothing Imogen could say would persuade the teenager otherwise, so she decided to give her the facts.

'What you are asking for is a very complex thing,' Imogen told her. 'Yes, it is done under certain circumstances, but only when the height of the person is such that they would be forever handicapped by it, or for health reasons. There are lots of teenagers as tall as you, and what you are asking for would mean the shortening of your leg bones. Tampering with healthy joints, weeks of discomfort, and all for what? The loss of a few inches?

'Go home and think about it very carefully. If you are still unhappy when you've done that, I can arrange for you to talk to a counsellor about your worries before recommending you to an orthopaedic consultant, who will almost certainly say the same as I have.'

The teenager went, still unconvinced, but her mother flashed Imogen a grateful smile.

There'd been a raised voice in the room next door during the morning, but the underlying calm tones of Blair had eventually seemed to have taken some of the heat out of the atmosphere.

'What was all that about?' Imogen asked when the waiting room had finally been cleared.

Blair sighed.

'Some guy who was getting all upset because the results of his wife's tests hadn't come through. I got the receptionist to chase them up and they should be here in the morning. He's normally the calmest of mortals but stress can do funny things to us and I'm afraid that family has some traumatic days ahead. I suspect that his wife might have lupus and it's not a pleasant complaint, as I'm sure you know.

'Which prompts me to say that if ever you experience any kind of aggression in the consulting room, ring for me. Violence towards doctors and nurses is becoming more prevalent all the time and it just won't do. Not in this place anyway.'

'I can look after myself, you know,' she told him.

'So you keep saying,' he commented drily, 'but nevertheless bear that in mind, will you? Turning to more mundane things, here's a list of calls. I've picked out those that should be relatively simple until you're more familiar with the patients, and when you've done them I suggest you grab a bite of lunch.'

She was ravenous and said, 'After? Not before?'

'Why, didn't you have any breakfast?'

Imogen wondered what he would say if she came out with the trite old phrase that she was eating for two. Quite a lot, she imagined, but that day had yet to come.

'The women patients are really pleased that we have a woman doctor in the practice again,' Lauren said when Imogen stopped at Reception before leaving on her rounds.

'That's good to know. Speaking of women doctors, Blair told me he'd once had a problem with a trainee GP. Do you know what that was all about?' she asked curiously. From what she'd seen so far of Blair Nesbitt, he didn't look like the sort of man who would let himself be intimidated by anyone.

Lauren looked around to make sure they weren't being overheard and said, 'She was a trainee from Aberdeen who was more tart than tartan and she was determined to get her claws into Blair. He didn't want to know and in the end had to tell her so, which made her turn spiteful. She accused him of falsifying prescriptions, neglecting his patients and every other misdemeanour she could think of. The practice was investigated but needless to say it was all proved to be lies and he sent her on her way.' Lauren looked at Imogen meaningfully. 'He's been wary of women ever since, but he seems quite keen on you.' She smiled. 'So what is it that you've got that others haven't?'

'Nothing that I can think of.'

'Except that you are every man's dream girl.'

Imogen grimaced.

'Time will tell but, take it from me, I'm more likely to turn out to be his nightmare than his dream girl.'

The fact that she was pregnant by a man who wasn't around any more would be seen by some as cause for sympathy, but others might construe her present state and her confident breezy nonchalance as an indication that she was free and easy with her favours.

Only she knew that she cried herself to sleep each night, and wasn't sure if her tears were for the dead Sean, herself or her fatherless child. She supposed they were for all three of them if the truth were known.

So far so good, Blair was thinking as he set off in the opposite direction to Imogen to do his own visits. Imogen had dealt with morning surgery in a cool and efficient manner. She'd turned up looking very smart and hadn't put a foot wrong so far. She was like her father in those respects, but for the rest she was an unknown quantity.

Did that matter, though? It was what she brought to the practice that mattered, not what was going on beneath that shiny dark hair. Had she a man in her life? he wondered. It would be incredible if she hadn't. Yet her down-to-earth manner could be offputting, he supposed.

As he pulled up in front of a home for the elderly he put thoughts of her to one side and went to seek out the sister in charge.

'It's George again, Doctor,' she said when he was shown into the office. 'He's wandered off three times today and the third time he fell and hurt his knee. We keep a close watch on him, but it isn't possible to have our eye on him all the time. Would you take a look at him?'

The old man in question could talk about some things with a mind as sharp as his own and at other times he was completely disorientated when blood flow to the brain was impeded.

'Yes of course, I'll take a look at the knee,' he told her. 'Where is he?'

The bony knee was bruised and swollen, and as Blair looked into watery blue eyes there was an emptiness there that told its own story.

The sister was hovering and he said, 'I think an X-ray just to be on the safe side. Have you someone free to take him? If not, send for an ambulance, Sister.'

She nodded and said, 'I think it might be something to do with thirst that causes him to wander. We found him in the White Lion with a gin and tonic in front of him.'

Blair laughed.

'So he coped with ordering that.'

'I think they know what he drinks. It was his local before he came in here.'

As Blair was leaving the home of a patient who had been sent home from hospital the previous day after surgery for a duodenal ulcer and was still getting discharge from the incision, a call came through from the police to ask if he would go to an alleyway in the city centre where the body of a man had been found.

'We tried Imogen Rossiter as she was nearest, but

she passed us on to you,' the police inspector said. 'Reckoned she wasn't feeling well.'

'Where was Dr Rossiter when you spoke to her?' he asked.

'In a lay-by somewhere.'

As he drove towards the place that the police had directed him to, Blair was frowning. He'd thought things had been going too well with Imogen. She'd seemed well enough when they'd parted company at the practice. What was going on?

When the call had come through Imogen had been vomiting. It was the first time that the queasiness had occurred later in the day and she'd thought it was typical that it should happen today of all days. She hoped that Blair wouldn't mind having the call-out passed on to him.

The man lying in the alleyway looked to be in his thirties. He'd been dead for some time as rigor mortis had set in. The police hadn't moved him. When they'd seen there was nothing they could do for him, they had left him where he was until cause of death had been established. Once the police surgeon had carried out his examination and the scene-of-crime officers had fulfilled their function, he would be taken to the mortuary.

He was lying on his side, revealing a gaping wound to the back of his head. His hands were clenched and as Blair knelt beside him he saw that he was holding something in one of them. A scrap of plastic was sticking out through his fingers.

Slowly removing it from the man's grip, he passed

a small packet containing a white substance to the police inspector.

The man sighed.

'I might have guessed. Dealer maybe, or user.'

'Looks like it,' Blair agreed as he continued his examination of the body.

When he'd finished he said, 'It's not clear whether the blow to the head actually killed him or if there was another contributing factor. I'd like to see what's going on underneath him as there has been some bleeding from underneath him.'

As he eased the body of the man onto its back he gave a nod of satisfaction. 'There it is.' He pointed to a neat round hole where the shirt was tucked into the jeans. 'He's been shot in the stomach.'

'There's a bullet casing somewhere around,' the inspector told his men. 'Get searching. Forensic will want to see it.' He turned to Blair who was getting to his feet. 'How long would you say he's been dead, Dr Nesbitt?'

'Difficult to tell,' Blair told him. 'The pathology boys will be able to be more accurate, but I'd say some time around the early hours of last night.'

All the way back to the practice Blair was wondering how Imogen was. If she'd managed to return to the Sycamores all right. And what was wrong with her. He'd asked her a couple of times if she was well and had been told firmly that she was fine. So where had today's malady come from?

When he passed the door of her consulting room she was perched on the corner of the desk, looking perfectly fit, with her long legs swinging as she tucked into a sandwich.

He took a step back and went in.

'So what was wrong with you earlier?' he asked curiously.

'I thought I was starting with a stomach upset,' she said with a twist of the truth. And giving colour to the statement, went on to say, 'I was struck by sudden awful nausea and pulled into a lay-by where I sat quietly until it subsided.'

'I see, but you are obviously all right now,' he commented, his eyes on the food in her hand and other delicacies on the desk beside her. 'What about the calls I asked you to do?'

'I've done them. I carried on as soon as I felt better.' Her smile was rueful and he had no idea of the panic she'd been in at the time as she said, 'Not a very prestigious beginning, was it? Feeling ill on my first day.'

Blair was observing her thoughtfully and he didn't return the smile.

'No, indeed. But as long as you're feeling better, that's the main thing. We've a couple of hours free before the late afternoon surgery so if you want to pop home or whatever, do so.'

Imogen shook her head.

'Thanks, but no. I'd like to help Dr Robertson with the antenatal clinic if I may. Once he's gone I imagine I'll be involved with the mothers-to-be, so I might as well get into the routine as soon as possible.'

'You presume rightly,' Blair said smoothly, 'however I was giving you time to settle in first. But if that's what you want, go ahead.'

Imogen was easing herself off the corner of the desk and bending to brush the crumbs off her skirt. When she straightened up their glances met and she knew he was having doubts about her.

'I'm sorry I had to pass the call from the police on

to you,' she said appeasingly. 'What did it turn out to be?'

'Murder. A shooting that was probably drugs-related. It would have done nothing to help the nausea you were experiencing,' he told her blandly, and again she had the feeling that Blair was having second thoughts about her.

CHAPTER THREE

DURING the next couple of weeks various things happened. To Imogen's relief the morning sickness eased off, as it often did as a pregnancy progressed.

Apart from it being something that would have drawn Blair's attention to her physical state if it had occurred while she'd been at the practice, there had also been the discomfort of it that had made her feel less than well each morning.

Another occurrence was a visit to the practice of her father and Celia, which was a far less welcome happening than the departure of the nausea.

When she heard her father's authoritative tones outside her consulting room one day out of surgery hours, her colour rose. She could hear Blair's voice mingling and that of Andrew Travis to a lesser degree, and she thought angrily that her father was here to check up on her.

The door opened and Blair was framed there, eyeing her mutinous expression quizzically.

'Your father's here,' he said in a low voice. 'Did you know? He's having a glass of sherry with Andrew at the moment.'

She nodded.

'I heard his voice. What's his excuse?'

'He's brought your stepmother to be taken on as a patient and before you get all steamed up, I believe that it was her idea to come. It's what she wants.'

Imogen had to smile.

'Wants? Or has been told that is how it has to be? It's one way of him keeping an eye on me. He's into surveillance in a big way.'

Blair was laughing openly now.

'I'm beginning to wonder if Emily Pankhurst has risen from the grave,' he said, and then on a more serious note, 'Are you going to have a word with them?'

She got to her feet slowly.

'I suppose so. I would do anything for Celia. She's kind and thoughtful and probably understands Dad a lot better than I ever will. I just hope he knows how lucky he is.'

'So shouldn't you be out catching criminals?' Imogen asked her father after she'd given Celia an affectionate hug.

He observed her unsmilingly.

'There are those beneath me paid to do that, Imogen. I've taken the morning off to bring Celia to be registered with this practice.'

'So it has nothing to do with me being employed here?'

'Not necessarily. She needed to register with someone in the area and as I'm already a patient it seemed the obvious thing to do.' He turned to Blair. 'So how is my daughter coping?'

I don't believe it, Imogen thought. Or maybe I do! He was discussing her as if she wasn't there. She found that she was holding her breath as she waited for Blair's reply.

'I feel that Dr Rossiter will be a great asset to the practice once she's settled in,' he told him with a gravity that belied the smile tugging at his mouth.

Blair could imagine how Imogen was feeling at that

moment. What was the old martinet like? He would have said what he had even if Imogen had been a flop, and she was far from that.

The chief constable cleared his throat.

'Good! Glad to hear it. The name of Rossiter is respected in the county.'

'Spare me!' Imogen gritted her teeth. What would he say about the Rossiter name when it was passed on to an illegitimate child?

When they'd gone Blair said, 'I'm sorry you had to put up with that.'

She sighed.

'It's the name of the game where my dad's concerned. I want to apologise for him turning up like that. He had no right.'

He saw that she looked pale and downcast and, wanting to bring back her zest, said, 'Don't give it another thought. I meant what I said, you know. It wasn't just for your father's benefit.'

Her face brightened.

'You did?'

'Of course. I never say what I don't mean.'

She was eyeing him thoughtfully and he wondered what was going through that mercurial mind of hers.

'You know, I can believe that. I wish I could say the same for myself,' she told him flatly.

Blair smiled.

'I would imagine that you're pretty straightforward in most things. You don't beat about the bush when you have something to say.'

Not always, she thought. He might be seeing her in a different light very soon, but she wouldn't be the first GP who'd carried on working while she was pregnant.

*   *   *

Imogen was getting to know Blair better as the days went by and the more she saw of him the more she liked what she saw.

Bill had gone and Andrew was taking a less active part in the practice with each passing day, so Blair and herself were the mainstays at the Sycamores.

Another happening during those first weeks at the practice was a visit from Blair's younger brother, a paler, less rugged version of the man himself. He breezed in one afternoon, took one look at her and flashed a friendly smile.

'I'm Simon Nesbitt,' he announced. 'And I take it that you are the new member of the practice.'

Imogen returned the smile with one of her own and held out a steady ringless hand.

'Yes. I'm Imogen Rossiter. Blair and I have both been out on calls and he isn't back yet. I don't think he'll be long if you'd like to wait.'

The young chef nodded.

'Sure. I'm in no hurry.'

He was observing her expectantly and Imogen wondered what was coming next.

'Is it true that you're a police surgeon like my brother and that your father's the chief constable?' he asked.

'Did Blair tell you that?' she questioned in return, wondering just what sort of a description he'd given of her to another member of his family.

Simon Nesbitt smiled again.

'Yes. It's not often he mentions anyone at the practice, and you didn't sound like the average GP, which made me think I'd come and see for myself.'

'So you're not here to see Blair?'

'I am partly. He left a note to say that he's bringing

someone to dine at the restaurant where I work tonight and I was curious to know who it is.'

That makes two of us, Imogen thought with no intention of letting him see that she was just as interested as he was.

At that moment Blair came striding into Reception. On seeing his brother and the latest addition to the practice engaged in conversation, he eyed them with raised brows and enquired abruptly, 'What's going on here?'

'I've been introducing myself to Imogen,' Simon said easily.

'But that's not the reason for you being here, I take it.'

'Not exactly. I came to ask who you are dining with tonight.'

'You'll have to wait and see,' Blair told him. 'I only mentioned it so that you wouldn't be too shocked to see me socialising for once.'

'So you're not going to tell me?'

'Not until I've extended the invitation. It might not materialise.'

'You're not bringing Briony Matthews, I hope,' Simon said in sepulchral tones. 'You know that the winsome widow has got you lined up for husband number two.'

Imogen was listening with a mixture of amusement and dismay. Yet why should she be upset to discover women in Blair Nesbitt's life? Just because he'd told her he had never found time to settle down, it didn't have to mean that he lived like a monk.

Ignoring the comment, Blair said in a milder tone, 'Haven't you got something better to do than frittering

away the afternoon here? Such as tidying up the sham-
bles that you've turned my spare room into?'

Simon pretended to shudder. 'Now you're upsetting
me.'

'Really?' Blair remarked drily. 'Well, you're going
to have to scoot anyway as Imogen and I have work
to do.'

Simon had been perched on the edge of her desk but
at that he got to his feet and, turning to her, said, 'Nice
to have met you, Dr Rossiter. Maybe we could get
together some time?'

'Thanks, but I don't think that would be possible,'
she told him with a smile. 'I'm rather committed at the
moment, but it's been very nice to meet you.'

On that note of gentle rebuff he went on his way,
leaving Imogen aware of her thickening waistline and
Blair to ponder over the 'commitments' that had suddenly appeared out of the blue.

Fond as he was of Simon, he'd been irritated to find
him chatting Imogen up. His presence at the practice
had been about as welcome as that of her father. And
the cheek of him to ask her out on such brief acquaintance.

His brother's unsociable hours of employment limited opportunities to meet the opposite sex...but really!
If anyone was going to be asking her out it was himself, and that was what he was planning to do. It was
Imogen that he intended taking to dine at the Belvedere
restaurant tonight if she would accept the invitation.

It would be an opportunity to ask how she felt about
the job. Was she settling in? That was the only reason
he was going to ask her out. It had nothing to do with
the fact that she fascinated him. Her smile. The turn of
her head. Her youthful independence. Everywhere he

went her face was before him. He'd been dazzled by her on that first night of meeting in the police station and so far nothing had changed.

He'd seen the question in Imogen's eyes when Simon had mentioned Briony Matthews. Blair could have throttled him. Briony had been married to a friend of his who'd been chairman of the local hospital trust and had turned to him when her husband had died suddenly.

But if she did have him earmarked as husband number two, she was wasting her time, he thought grimly. She was elegant, wealthy and beginning to be somewhat possessive when they were in each other's company, so he wasn't intending letting that state of affairs continue.

He could have kicked himself for not having suggested the evening out to Imogen earlier in the day, but it had been one of those mornings with not a moment to spare and now his young brother had blundered in first.

'So you're out on the town tonight,' she said brightly as the thoughts raced through his mind.

'I'm not sure,' he replied slowly. 'It all depends if you're free and would like to dine with me at the Belvedere where Simon works.'

Imogen felt her jaw go slack.

'Me!'

'Yes, you. It's some weeks since you joined us here and I thought it would give me a chance to show you just how much I appreciate your contribution to the practice. So what do you say?'

'I'd love to,' she breathed, adding with her usual candour, 'it's ages since I went anywhere exciting.'

'You surprise me. I don't see you in the Cinderella

guise. What about the commitments that you mentioned to that impudent brother of mine?'

'Oh, I was merely referring to my police surgeon duties and the job here,' she told him airily.

'So you're not with anyone?'

He watched her face cloud over.

'No. No I'm not.'

Imogen thought she saw relief in his eyes but it gave her no pleasure. She supposed she really *was* 'with someone', but not in the way he'd meant. The foetus that she was carrying was going to be the biggest commitment she was ever likely to make and she was pretty scared about what lay ahead.

'What time shall I pick you up?' Blair was asking.

'Eight o'clock?'

He nodded.

'Right. I'll go and make a reservation now.'

When he'd gone Imogen sank down into the chair behind the desk and let relief and quick pleasure wash over her at the thought of the evening ahead. They were happy emotions and yet she felt like weeping.

She'd made the grade and Blair was taking her out to celebrate. Both reasons for delight. But if he was so satisfied with her, wasn't now the time to tell him about the baby? That was the deal she'd made with her conscience. That once she'd made herself indispensable and was happy she could carry on throughout her pregnancy, she would tell him…before nature did it for her.

Was tonight going to have to be confession time, when all she wanted was to enjoy his company and bask in his praise? But any further mental debate on that problem had to be postponed as the mothers were arriving for the weekly antenatal clinic and the rest of the afternoon was taken up with the affairs of those in a similar condition to herself.

Her own antenatal checks were being carried out in the privacy of her apartment and so far there were no problems in that area.

She noticed that there seemed to be an equal proportion of married and unmarried mothers amongst those attending the clinic, but the single ones all appeared to have partners in the background or some other kind of family backing, while in her own life there was no one.

Celia wouldn't condemn her when she knew, but whether she would support her against her father Imogen wasn't sure, and the thought of how he would react made her break out in a sweat every time she considered it. Unlike Blair, she had no siblings to turn to either, so she was preparing for it to be 'go it alone' time when the baby arrived.

As the practice nurse checked blood pressures and urine samples, Imogen examined the patients one by one. Obviously they were all at different stages of pregnancy. Some, like herself, were in the early stages. Others were further on, and a couple of mothers-to-be were about to give birth in the very near future.

In the case of one of them, her blood pressure had soared since the previous week and Imogen had no choice but to tell her that she would have to be admitted to hospital immediately. It was a first, much-longed-for baby for a couple in their early forties, and she wasn't taking any chances.

The woman's colour drained from her face when she was told that the receptionist was going to phone for an ambulance to come directly to the surgery.

'Is it that serious?' she asked anxiously.

Imogen's smile flashed out.

'Not if we get you into bed rest under hospital supervision immediately,' she told her. 'You've three weeks to go and will probably be kept in until the birth.'

She picked up the phone and handed it to her.

'You can call your husband from here and ask him to meet you at the hospital with whatever you might need in clothes and toiletries.'

'Have you got any children, Doctor?' the woman asked as they waited for the ambulance to arrive.

'No, not as yet,' Imogen told her, and with the thought of Blair within earshot refrained from adding, But I soon will have.

As she dressed for the dinner date with Blair, Imogen was wishing that he'd asked her out for a different reason. Not because he felt bound to do the honours for a satisfactory member of staff, but because he desired her company in the way of a man who saw a woman that he wanted to be with.

She was strongly attracted to him and wished she wasn't. To fall in love with Blair Nesbitt would only complicate her life further. If he returned her feelings it would be fantastic, but it went without saying that he would have second thoughts when he found out she was pregnant from a previous relationship. It would be certain to put the blight on any chemistry between them.

At the back of her mind there was always the thought that if Sean hadn't gone cavorting off to the Himalayas, none of it would be happening. She would still be working in Birmingham, though whether he would still have been on the scene she didn't know.

Deep down inside her there was a feeling that maybe the fates hadn't been too unkind. If things hadn't happened the way they had, she would never have met Blair, and as she paused in front of the mirror for a final glance before going to let him into the apartment, she knew that whatever the future held she wouldn't have wanted to miss that.

'Whew!' Blair said when he saw her. 'Can this be the restrained dresser who occupies the consulting room next to mine? If Simon manages to escape from the kitchen while we're at the Belvedere, he really will be on the scent.'

'I haven't dressed for Simon,' she told him meaningfully. 'I'm only interested in your approval.'

'You have it,' he said as the warmth in his eyes deepened.

'Let's go, then,' she suggested, satisfied that if she hadn't made an impression on him previously, she had tonight.

The sleeveless dress of pale turquoise silk with matching three-quarter-length jacket made her smooth skin glow and the dark lustre of her hair stand out against its shimmering lines. Now that the sickness had passed, her face had filled out and tonight there was a radiance about her that Blair hadn't seen before. He wasn't to know that it was a case of one last fling for Imogen before her big confession.

'Ooh! This is nice,' Imogen said as a waiter showed them to a table in the Belvedere restaurant which was fast becoming one of the city's most exclusive eating places. 'What exactly does Simon do here?'

'He's a chef. He went to catering college and after working in kitchens lower down the scale has landed himself a job here. He's good. Always had a natural talent for cooking. He's usually kept busy behind the scenes but what's the bet he has a quick peep to see who I'm with?'

'So he doesn't know it's me. He mentioned someone else that he thought you might be dining with, didn't he?'

Blair smiled.

'Yes. I sometimes take the widow of a friend of mine out for a meal. Simon doesn't approve. I think that he sees himself having nowhere to live if I were to marry Briony Matthews.'

'And is that likely?' she asked as her palms became moist and her throat went dry.

'What? That he would have nowhere to live?'

'No. That you might marry this woman?'

Was he being deliberately evasive?

'I have no plans of that nature at the moment,' he said briefly, and she had to be satisfied with that.

As the evening progressed Imogen gave herself up to enjoyment. Soon, like Cinderella, she would have to go dismally home, knowing that the magical night had been exactly that. A one-off occasion.

It would be Blair's esteem that she was losing rather than a glass slipper, yet the effect would be just as disastrous. But in the meantime she was going to make the most of this time together. Maybe she could charm him into forgiving her deception.

Imogen was certainly charming, Blair thought as the evening ticked away. She was getting to him. His blood warmed every time their eyes met. His pulses were racing. His heartbeat quickening. Was she the one he'd been waiting for all this time? Someone he would want to be the mother of his children?

Her every word, look, gesture was mesmerising. He'd known the moment he'd seen her in the police station that night that it was fate. He'd invited her to join the practice against his better judgement and it had worked out fine. It was meant that they should be together.

The meal was almost over. They were enjoying coffee when his mobile rang. He listened for a moment and then said, 'Can't you get hold of someone else? I'm in the middle of an evening out.'

Blair sighed. He didn't believe this. His presence was required by the city police, just as the magical evening with Imogen was at its peak.

'All right. I'll be there as soon as I can,' he agreed sombrely, as he was informed that he was the only one they'd been able to get hold of.

As he replaced the phone in his jacket pocket he met her questioning hazel gaze.

'What's wrong?' she asked.

'A suspicious death. The police have just pulled a body out of the canal.'

'I'll come with you.'

Blair eyed her in surprise.

'No need. I'll drop you off home first.'

Imogen shook her head.

'I'd rather be in on it with you. For one thing you're the most experienced of the police surgeons on the rota, so it will do me good to watch you in action…and for another I don't want the evening to end.'

'Neither do I,' he told her huskily, and took her arm. 'So let's go and see what they've got for us.'

He was smiling as the car pulled away from the side of the restaurant.

'The police said they'd tried to get hold of you but you weren't around so they'll be surprised when we turn up together. It will either set tongues wagging or they'll take it for granted we've been on another job together.'

'I imagine you wouldn't like that,' she remarked.

'What?'

'Tongues wagging.'

'It would depend on what they were wagging about,' he said blandly, as he swerved to avoid a car coming out of a side street.

The body of a man had been pulled out of the canal soon after darkness had fallen over the city. It was a recently renovated waterfront with a smattering of apartments and bars that would be crowded as the area's night life took over, but at the time of the discovery of the corpse the area had been almost deserted.

'We received an anonymous call to say that there was a body in the canal,' the police officer in charge told them. 'When we got here he was floating face down, but we don't think he'd been in the water long.'

He pointed to the nearest bar.

'One of the staff in that place heard a cry and a scuffle earlier on, but as they were busy getting set up for the evening trade he didn't take much notice. He reckons that kind of thing goes on all the time.'

As the two police surgeons bent over the inert figure he informed them, 'There was no pulse or heartbeat and resuscitation had no effect.'

Blair was eyeing the body consideringly.

'If there was alcohol present and he stumbled into

the water, his reflexes wouldn't have been as sharp. Also he would have had a better chance if he'd been floating face up. In most cases of drowning, when the person starts taking in small amounts of water the laryngeal reflex, an automatic contraction of muscles at the entrance to the windpipe, directs the water to the oesophagus and stomach instead of into the lungs. But it can obstruct breathing which soon brings about unconsciousness.

'However, if the person is still buoyant at that time and facing upwards, the muscles begin to relax and normal breathing may recommence. In this instance the odds are that he fell forward and remained in that position all the time he was in the water.

'What do you think, Dr Rossiter?' he asked his companion, giving her the opportunity to vouchsafe an opinion. 'Are we looking at a suicide, foul play or an accident?'

Imogen didn't answer immediately. She was observing the body with a thoughtful stare.

'I've seen this guy somewhere before. I recognise the clothes and that strange ring on his hand. It's the fellow who'd had the epileptic fit in the cells on the night we met.'

The two men were eyeing her in surprise.

'Are you sure?' Blair asked.

'Yes,' she told him firmly.

'Well, in that case,' he told the policeman, 'you won't have any trouble identifying him. They'll have his name and address at the central police station where Dr Rossiter attended him. He was arrested a few weeks ago for assaulting his ex-wife's new boyfriend. So it could be suicide, or the other fellow getting his own back, or even something different altogether.'

'Such as him having an epileptic seizure while beside the canal?' Imogen suggested.

Blair had finished examining the body and as he got to his feet he said, 'There is a swelling above the temple which concerns me. If the victim fell in head first, or even sideways, I can't see him banging his head on the bank, or anywhere else for that matter. Unless he hit debris that was already in the water. Or had already been struck before he fell in the canal.'

'The man was in a dreadful state on the night he was arrested,' Imogen reminded him. 'It wouldn't be surprising if he'd decided to end it all, but that wouldn't allow for the blow to the head, would it?'

Blair nodded and, turning to the policeman, said, 'I'll speak to the pathology people and tell them what we've found and put them in the picture with regard to what Dr Rossiter knows of his domestic and health problems. You can move him now.'

As he drove Imogen home a little later Blair was conscious that the depressing incident they'd had to participate in had wiped out the sparkle of the night.

Before the phone call had brought him down to earth he'd been in a state of entrancement. Wanting to touch her, hold her, kiss the mobile mouth in that captivating face.

Maybe it had done him a favour, the voice of reason said. He'd only known Imogen a short time. Not long enough to be going overboard with crazy longing. He knew nothing about her past and only what he'd seen so far about her present.

She was a good doctor, daughter of the chief constable and had cast a spell over him, he thought with a quick glance at her profile in the shadowed confines of the car.

Aware of his gaze, Imogen asked, 'What are you thinking?'

She knew it would be nothing like her own thoughts, which were centring around a confession that had been postponed. But she certainly wasn't expecting him to say what he did.

'I was wondering if we could take up where we left off before duty called,' he said in a low voice. 'How about asking me up for coffee?'

'Yes, why not?' she agreed with a suicidal smile. It had to be done so why not tell Blair about the baby in the privacy of her own home?

But the moment the door had closed behind them she found herself in his arms. Looking deep into her eyes, he said, 'You know that I'm not bothered about coffee, don't you, Imogen? That I want to make love to you. Tell me that you feel the same.'

There was a pain around her heart as if a knife had sliced into it, and tears welled up in her eyes. In different circumstances she would have melted at his touch. Told him joyously that she did feel the same. But how could she?

Unaware of the pain inside her, his arms had tightened. Holding her against the hard wall of his chest, he kissed her yearning mouth.

It would be so easy to give in to the moment, Imogen thought weakly as she kissed him back with brief, fierce longing. But reason was lurking. Common sense was ready to pounce, and if she hadn't been honest with Blair before she knew that she had to be now.

'Don't, Blair,' she begged against the mouth that was laying claim to hers.

His arms slackened, and he became still.

'What is it?' he asked slowly. 'I thought…'

She took his hand and drew him towards the sofa.

'I have something to tell you,' she said in a low voice.

With the passion draining from him like water down the sink, he prompted, 'What?'

'I'm pregnant.'

'Wha-at?' he cried. 'Who by? Why have you not mentioned it before?'

The questions were coming at her like bullets.

'I wanted a little time in the job before I told you. In six months the pregnancy will be over and lots of women doctors work while they are carrying.'

'Well, yes, of course they do,' he agreed, still in a state of amazement.

'But, Imogen, I'm angry that you let me make a fool of myself before telling me what's going on in your life. Who's the father?'

'His name is…was…Sean Derwent.'

Blair hated seeing her so chastened. It had been Imogen's zest and vibrance that he'd been attracted to.

But what was it that she'd just said? That Sean something or other was the child's father and she had spoken as if he was no longer around. Had the rat deserted her when he'd found out?

'So he's in the past, then, this Sean guy?' he questioned tightly.

Imogen had turned away, slender shoulders drooping.

'Yes. He's in the past. He's dead, Blair.'

'Oh, hell! What a mess!'

'Yes, isn't it?' she said wearily. 'I know I should have told you right from the beginning but I needed to prove to myself that I could pull my weight while I was pregnant.'

'So you decided to deceive me,' he commented flatly.

'I didn't lie, Blair,' she said pleadingly. 'I just kept quiet.'

'And let me make a prize fool of myself tonight into the bargain.'

She was beginning to fight back.

'This was to be my last night of being well thought of by you. I'd intended telling you in the restaurant but—'

'You got a reprieve?'

'Yes.'

'And so what would you have done if I hadn't asked myself up for coffee? Put it off until you had no choice in the matter?'

'I don't know,' she told him. 'I've been dreading this moment, because even though we haven't known each other long I value your respect. I don't suppose that you ever do anything you're ashamed of.'

He almost smiled.

'Don't start trying to get round me. Of course I do things that I regret. We all do. I'm just sorry that it's taken you so long to tell me something I would have been happier to have known from the beginning. But at least, now that I do know, I can do some rearranging of my feelings, which I won't allow to get out of hand again in a hurry.'

He was turning to go but had one last thing to say.

'I'm sorry that the man who made you pregnant is dead. That is very sad for both you and the child.'

As Imogen opened her mouth to tell him the circumstances of Sean's death, he held up his hand.

'I've heard enough for one night, Imogen. Don't say anything else.' And on that final note he left.

CHAPTER FOUR

WHEN Blair arrived back at his own place he sat inside his car, staring into space. He was devastated. For the first time in years he'd been on the brink of falling in love. Enchanted by a woman who was carrying another man's child—only he hadn't known that.

It wasn't Imogen's fault that he'd felt the way he had. She hadn't deliberately set out to attract him, but attract him she had, and now he felt sick in his stomach after the night's revelations.

Why in the name of glory hadn't she told him the truth at the beginning? he thought raggedly. And where did they go from here? Nowhere. If he took any notice of common sense.

He was a doctor, for heaven's sake, only too acutely aware that nature hadn't balanced the scales evenly when it came to the business of child-bearing.

It was the woman's body that was fashioned to carry the foetus, the woman who bore the pain during child-birth, and in situations where she was left to cope alone there wasn't always the support and sympathy she deserved. It was so easy to make a child, but the act in itself could change her life forever.

Yet had he remembered that tonight when he'd been ranting on at Imogen? No, he hadn't. He'd let disappointment and pique make him less than the charitable person that he was.

Tomorrow he would ask her what had happened to her child's father and how much he'd meant to her.

One thing he wouldn't be discussing was what had been in his heart earlier.

Imogen's place in his life had changed in the space of a few hours. She was still the desirable woman who had made his pulses race as they'd never done before. Still the enchantress who had lit up his life from the moment of meeting.

But he'd discovered that she was carrying another man's child. Everything had changed, even though the Sean person was dead. And what state did that leave him in?

He was jealous, for one thing. Wished that the child was his.

Angry? Only to the extent that she'd kept it from him when he would rather have known.

Hurting? Oh, yes! Because he didn't spread his affections around carelessly. Yet how could Imogen have known what his feelings for her were before tonight? She did now, though. In the space of minutes she'd discovered that he was attracted to her and then had had to watch that attraction wiped out by disbelief.

When Simon's car pulled up beside his an eternity later, his young brother came across and knocked on the window. As Blair wound it down he said, 'What are you doing out here? Dreaming about Imogen? I saw the two of you in the restaurant. You're the crafty one, aren't you? Letting me come on to her when you had designs on her yourself.'

Blair sighed.

'You've got it all wrong, Simon. I'll tell you about it some time.'

So that was that, Imogen thought dismally as she lay sleepless between the sheets. It had ended as she'd known it would, with Blair angry at being kept in the dark and the magical thing that had been happening between them shattered into a thousand pieces.

But as the moments passed pride resurfaced. If Blair's opinion of her had dropped to zero, so be it. If she had hurt him emotionally and made working together difficult then first thing in the morning she would hand in her notice.

She supposed that now her secret was out of the bag she might as well tell her father and have done with it. He wouldn't be able to make her feel any worse than Blair had. At least she wouldn't have to concern herself about her changing shape once he had also been put in the picture.

Blair was already at his desk when Imogen arrived for morning surgery the next day and, like a patient wanting to get down a dose of nasty medicine as quickly as possible, she went straight into his office.

'I'm handing in my notice,' she said with flat brevity. 'I'm sure that's what you'd like me to do.'

'And since when have you thought yourself able to read my mind?' he asked with a quick glance at the shadows beneath her eyes.

'Since last night when I told you I was pregnant and you made your thoughts on the matter crystal clear,' she retorted.

He pointed to the chair that was normally occupied by his patients. 'Sit down, Imogen, before you fall down. I don't want your notice.'

'Why?'

'Because I want you to stay. I said things last night that I shouldn't have and I'm sorry.'

She was observing him with amazed hazel eyes.

'So you're not condemning me?'

'Of course not. My anger last night was because you hadn't been straight with me, but, as I've just said, I can understand why.'

He cleared his throat. 'With regard to what happened between us before that, it would never have occurred if I'd known the circumstances. Obviously it won't happen again.'

Her heart sank. So that was to be it. He'd accepted her pregnancy but it had put her out of bounds as far as he was concerned on a personal level.

Well, she supposed that she should be grateful for that. She would still see him each day at the practice if nowhere else.

'So, are you going to take off your jacket and let us both get the day under way?' he suggested, and she smiled.

'Yes, I'll do that.' She flashed him a smile. 'I'm going to tell my dad now that you know and get all my confessions out of the way.'

As she turned to go he said, 'One last thing, and then the subject is closed. How did your child's father die?'

'He was killed in a freak storm on Everest...not knowing he'd made me pregnant.'

'That must have been dreadful.'

'Yes, it was,' she told him levelly.

There was no point in informing him that it had also been the first and last time she'd made love with Sean, and that she doubted if she would have wanted to marry him if he'd still been around.

Blair wouldn't want to hear that after what he'd said earlier. And could she blame him? Few men would want a relationship with a woman who was pregnant with another man's child.

If she'd had any doubts on that score, what Blair had to say later in the morning would have dispensed with them.

Surgery was over and Imogen was on the phone to the maternity wing of the city's biggest hospital, enquiring about the patient that she'd sent in the previous day with dangerously high blood pressure.

She wouldn't normally have followed up a referral to hospital but, being pregnant herself and knowing how much the couple wanted the child that they were expecting late in life, she'd felt bound to enquire about the condition of the mother-to-be.

It was as she'd expected. The blood pressure was coming down with bed rest and medication, but her patient would be kept in hospital until it was time for the birth.

As she replaced the phone Blair came in and closed the door behind him.

'Do you mind if I tell Simon about your pregnancy?' he asked.

'Er...no. But why?'

'He saw us last night at the Belvedere and jumped to his own conclusions. When he came home I explained that there wasn't going to be anything between us, and it has occurred to me since that he might see that as a signal to follow up the play he made for you yesterday...which could be embarrassing for you both.'

She supposed his thinking was logical enough, but for some reason Imogen was angry. Perhaps it was because of the bland way that he was making sure she knew he'd given up on her.

'Maybe I could carry a bell and cry, "Leper",' she

said tartly. 'Would that be sufficient to keep men away? Or will my spreading waistline be enough?'

Blair's face had straightened.

'I thought you might still be mourning the death of your child's father, and as I've already unwittingly intruded into that part of your life, I wouldn't want Simon to do the same.'

Imogen sighed.

'Tell him, Blair. Tell who you like. It doesn't matter. Only leave me to tell my father. It will be bad enough coming from me, but if he heard it from anyone else I shudder to think what might happen.'

'I'll come with you if you like,' he offered.

'What? I couldn't let you do that. I'm not a child.'

'I know that, but someone has to look after you, Imogen,' he said gently.

It was the gentleness that did it. Suddenly she was weeping. Tears for Sean, the baby and for what might have been between herself and Blair.

'Come here,' he said in the same soft tone, and as he held out his arms she went into them like a hurt animal.

'I'm going with you when you go to see your father, whether you want me to or not,' he said as she sobbed out all the pent-up misery. 'The chief constable is someone I wouldn't like to have to put in his place, but I will if I have to.'

That brought a smile amongst the tears.

'That would be a first. No one puts a foot wrong with my dad.'

'Yes, well, we'll have to wait and see what he says, won't we?' he said with an answering smile.

At that moment there were footsteps in the passage

outside and Andrew called, 'Are you there, Blair? I need a quick word.'

Blair moved quickly towards the door. 'Stay there until you feel better,' he said in a low voice. 'I'll head Andrew off.'

Imogen's first house visit of the day was to the home of an elderly couple. The wife had rung in the lunch-hour to say that she thought her eighty-year-old husband was having a mini-stroke.

'He's not talking sense,' she said agitatedly when Imogen arrived, 'and he keeps dribbling from the mouth.'

The young doctor nodded when she saw him. 'Yes. It would appear that your husband has had a minor stroke. As is the case when this happens, depending on which side of the brain is affected, the patient either loses the power of speech or is left with restricted movement. I'm going to test his blood pressure first and put him on some immediate medication.'

The man's speech improved while his blood pressure was being checked, and his wife gave a sigh of relief.

It was high, but not dangerously so, and Imogen told her, 'It would appear that there was a temporary block-age in an artery, but I can't guarantee that it won't happen again. Send for me immediately if he has an-other attack, and in the meantime I'll give you a pre-scription that has a similar effect to aspirin but without the risk of abdominal upset.'

When she arrived back at the practice she rang her father's house and Celia answered.

'Imogen!' she cried. 'When are you coming to see us?'

'One night this week if it's convenient,' she informed her stepmother.

'Yes, of course,' Celia said immediately. 'We've no engagements, so whenever it suits you will be fine by us.'

'Tomorrow, then?'

'Yes. You must eat with us.'

'Is it all right if I bring someone with me?'

'Of course. Can I ask who?' Celia probed.

'Blair Nesbitt.'

'Oh! Really! Your father will be pleased about that.'

'Don't get any wrong ideas, Celia,' she said quickly. 'Blair is just a friend.'

And there was nothing truer than that, she thought glumly as the practice nurse appeared in a state of some agitation to say that one of the receptionists was being harassed by a patient.

'Where are Blair and Andrew?' Imogen asked as she hurried towards Reception.

'I don't know,' the nurse said. 'They were here a moment ago.'

'What's the problem?' Imogen asked coolly of the man who was shouting abuse at the receptionist.

'She won't give me an appointment to see a doctor,' he bellowed, 'and I'm not going until she does!'

The receptionist was Lauren. Trying to make herself heard above his shouting, she said, 'He's drunk, Imogen. I've told him to come back when he's sober.'

'You heard what the receptionist said,' she told him. 'Do as she says.'

His attention had turned to herself now and he lunged towards her, sending her flying with his forearm.

She staggered back against the desk but fortunately

didn't lose her balance, and as she stood swaying from the force of the blow the man was gripped from behind by an enraged Blair.

'Look after Dr Rossiter,' he told Lauren as he pinned the man up against the wall. Addressing Andrew, who was dithering nearby, he said, 'Call the police, Andrew. This guy needs locking up until the beer's stopped talking.'

The police had been and taken the offender away. The nurse had bathed Imogen's face and made her a cup of hot sweet tea and now she was insisting that she was all right.

It was the first day of the rest of his life without Imogen and already he'd held her sobbing in his arms, offered his moral support when she went to face her father and been consumed by blind rage when he'd seen that fellow's arm come out to hit her. So much for keeping at a distance, Blair thought.

The chief constable's daughter was many things. Vulnerable, independent, reckless, clever...and achingly beautiful. And he was going to have to stand by and watch while she had another man's child.

How much had he meant to her? he wondered. This fellow who'd died on Everest? Had he been the love of her life?

As Imogen wandered restlessly around the apartment that night she couldn't stop thinking about the strange day that was drawing to a close.

It had begun with Blair telling her he wanted her to stay in the practice. An amazing thing in itself after his reaction of the previous night. Then he had dumbfounded her by offering to be present when she told her father about the baby and, immediately on top of that, she'd found herself in his arms sobbing her heart out.

And if all that hadn't been strange enough, there'd been his fury at the way the drunken man had hit her. She knew he would have been outraged to see any member of his staff being treated like that, but it had been almost as if she belonged to him.

She wished she did. She wished that she'd never met Sean. But the die had been cast in the form of an innocent baby that hadn't asked to be conceived.

Every caring thing Blair had done or said during the day had made her realise even more what a mess she'd made of her life. Imogen was beginning to feel it would be easier to bear if he'd stayed angry with her.

But one thing wasn't going to change. He was seeing her in a different light now. She'd become someone that he wasn't going to be able to rely on completely during the coming months with regard to the practice, and away from it he would see her as a woman with a function to fulfil that was going to keep them apart.

So what was she going to do? She was going to get on with her life, she thought rebelliously.

Her father was actually smiling when Imogen and Blair arrived at his house the following evening, and she read his mind immediately. He was thinking that for once she was doing the sensible thing if she'd taken up with Blair.

Her spirits sank even lower than they already were as he gave her a peck on the cheek and shook hands cordially with her companion.

When her father discovered that Blair was only there to give her support, the fat really would be in the fire.

But as yet he didn't know the reason for the visit and, not wanting to take away his appetite, she wasn't going to say anything until after they'd eaten.

The conversation during dinner was pleasant enough, with Blair and her father chatting about their affairs and Celia and herself enjoying their own conversation, but when they were settled with coffee in the sitting room afterwards Imogen knew she must wait no longer.

'I have something to tell you both,' she said, trying to sound cool.

Her father smiled and with a glance at Blair sitting beside her said, 'I hope it's what I think it is.'

'I'm afraid that you're in for a disappointment,' she told him. 'I'm pregnant.'

As she watched, the smile disappeared and the look she knew so well took its place. Disapproval, exasperation, annoyance were all there as he said, 'Couldn't you have waited until you married?' He turned to Blair. 'I'm disappointed in you, Nesbitt. Making my daughter pregnant without a wedding ring on her finger!'

Imogen was eyeing him in slow horror. She hadn't been wrong. He was jumping to conclusions. Her father was taking it for granted that because Blair was with her he was the father. She wanted to crawl into the nearest hole and hide herself away.

But she wasn't going to be able to do that. She had to put him right. Blair would just love having his good name dragged through the mire!

As she moistened dry lips to say her piece, the chief constable growled, 'I hope that you're going to do the honourable thing, Nesbitt.'

The situation was developing into a farce, she

thought hysterically as Blair replied, 'I wouldn't be here if I wasn't...sir.'

He didn't meet her eyes as she swung round to face him and as if from somewhere far away she heard her father's voice saying in a more placatory tone, 'Well, I suppose that's something. Er...how far into the pregnancy are you, Imogen?'

'Not far,' she croaked, 'but you don't understand... I have to explain.'

'There's no need, Imogen,' Blair said smoothly. 'I'm sure that your father will be happy to leave it to us to sort things out.'

She swallowed hard. Was he crazy?

'Yes, and without delay if you don't mind,' her parent said. 'Let's have a wedding to give some degree of respectability to it.'

'I only told Blair that I was pregnant a couple of days ago,' she told him protestingly, conscious that if nothing else was what it seemed, that at least was true.

'That's typical of you, Imogen,' he snapped, but before he could berate her further Celia butted in.

'It's wonderful news, Imogen, dear,' she said gently, and turned to Blair. 'She's a lovely girl, this stepdaughter of mine. You're a lucky man, Blair. Congratulations to you both.'

Linking her arm in her husband's, she looked up at the tall unrelenting figure and told him, 'Rejoice, my dear. You're going to be a grandfather.' And for the first time since he'd heard about his daughter's pregnancy Brian Rossiter smiled.

'So how about that for taking the wind out of the old tyrant's sails?' Blair said when they'd said their goodbyes later in the evening and were driving back to Imogen's apartment.

She'd been silent since leaving her father's house, speechless for once at the way the evening had turned out, but now she found her tongue.

'What about me?' she cried. 'How do you think I felt when you said what you did? I thought that by now it would be over. My dad would know I was pregnant and would have to accept it. But you've made things ten times more complicated, Blair. What's he going to say when he finds out that you're not the baby's father?'

'He's not going to. Not from me anyway.'

'I...don't...understand,' she said slowly. 'Do you realise what you're saying?'

'Yes.'

'You're going to let everyone think the baby's yours.'

'If it will make your life easier...yes.'

'It won't!' she cried. 'I'll know that it's not true and I'll feel guilty all the time because you're saddling yourself with me and my child for some crazy, chivalrous idea of your own.'

'Will you please calm down?' he said, stopping the car by the side of the road. 'I said what I did on impulse. Your father misunderstood why I was with you and, as I'm fancy-free and couldn't stand by and let him make mincemeat out of you, the opportunity was there to get him off your back and I took it.'

Imogen was rocking to and fro in the car seat.

'Yes, but words are dangerous things. Once said they can't be taken back. He's expecting a wedding.'

'So we'll give him one.'

She could feel her jaw dropping.

'You're not serious!'

'I've already explained once that I don't say things I don't mean.'

'I think I'm going to faint,' she said weakly.

Blair laughed. 'No, you're not. But I'll tell you what you are going to do. You're going to tell me if you want to go ahead with this marriage of convenience. If you don't, then, yes, I will tell your father that I was stringing him along. If you do, then we let matters rest and make our plans. So what do you say, Imogen?'

Still in a state of complete shock, she fixed him with her wide hazel gaze and thought that she was half in love with him already. It wouldn't take much to make her go all the way. But did she want a loveless marriage? Pity from a man who if he wanted could pick and choose when it came to her sex and might come to regret having made the gesture?

'I say yes,' she said slowly. 'On one condition. That we each leave the other free to go their own way in the future if they want to.'

For a moment she thought he was startled, but it passed and he said smoothly, 'Right. Agreed. Tomorrow we'll buy you a ring and then we'll have a look at some four-bedroomed houses. Simon will be delighted to find that he's going to have my apartment all to himself.'

'Why four-bedroomed houses?' she asked, still in the same slow tone of bemusement.

'One for me, one for you, one for the baby and a guest room.'

'Yes, I see,' she said flatly. He couldn't have put it any plainer than that.

When they reached her apartment Blair stayed in the car. 'Don't lie awake all night, thinking about it,' he

said, winding down the window. 'If you have any concerns, we'll discuss them tomorrow.'

She nodded and, still dazed and unbelieving, went
inside.

If Blair had been relaxed while he'd been with Imogen,
he was in a more sombre mood after he'd left her. He'd
told her that he'd misled Brian on impulse. But if he
was honest he had to admit that claiming to be the
father of Imogen's child had already been a half-
formed idea in his mind before she'd told the older
couple her news. And once she'd done so, the chief
constable's reaction had turned it into reality.

But was Imogen falling in with the idea willingly?
he asked himself. She'd been quick to stipulate that
they should each have an escape route, which he supposed was on a par with his allocation of the bedrooms.
It was a pretty loveless arrangement all round.

Yet he'd known that he wanted to take care of her
the previous day when she'd wept in his arms.
Suddenly it hadn't mattered that another man had made
her pregnant. She was young and impetuous…and
beautiful. And if she wanted to mourn the other guy,
it would be only natural.

He accepted that the idea of them getting married
was crazy. They barely knew each other. But it hadn't
stopped him from suggesting it. A smile tugged at his
lips. If he was willing to put up with old Rossiter for
a father-in-law, he really must be insane.

Imogen was no doormat, far from it, but dealing with
her father was like stumbling into a chamber of horrors.
In future the autocratic policeman would have himself
to deal with first when he wanted to get heavy-handed
with his daughter.

And now, as he paused outside Simon's door, he was about to contradict what he'd told his brother the night before. From assuring him that there was nothing between Imogen and himself, he was about to go to the other extreme by telling him that he was marrying her. And when Simon heard about the pregnancy he would jump to the same conclusion as everyone else.

'I'm not surprised,' Lauren said after Blair had made a brief announcement about the forthcoming wedding to the staff the following morning. 'Dr Nesbitt hasn't been able to take his eyes off you from the first day you came here.'

Imogen managed a smile.

'That wasn't love. It was because he wasn't sure about me. He'd taken me on against his better judgement.'

'Well, whatever it was, you've obviously passed the test,' the other woman said laughingly, 'and I'm sure that you'll be very happy together.'

Fighting off the feeling of unreality that was covering her like a cloak, Imogen gave her a squeeze and said, 'It will only be a quiet wedding as I'm pregnant, but will you be my bridesmaid?'

'Of course,' Lauren said enthusiastically, and with a meaningful glance out of the window at Simon, who had just pulled up outside, continued, 'I've never been a bridesmaid or a bride, but I'm working on it and what better set-up than to have a husband who's a chef? Simon comes in here frequently for one thing or another and we have a lot in common.'

Imogen laughed. 'If that's the way your mind's working, we'll be ending up related.'

'Can you spare a minute?' Simon asked her when he came through the door.

Lauren excused herself and Imogen observed him warily. The look on his face told her that Blair had put him in the picture.

'I don't know what your game is, Dr Rossiter,' he said in a low voice, 'but don't mess Blair about. They don't come any better than my older brother, and I can't believe that he's made you pregnant. He doesn't sleep around and he's a doctor, for goodness' sake. But, then, so are you, I suppose. If you're foisting some other man's child off on to him, you have some nerve.'

She wanted to defend herself against the accusation, but how could she because she was doing exactly that? Would he believe her if she told him that the whole idea had been Blair's? He might, but Simon could still come back at her by telling her she could have said no.

Instead, she told him coolly. 'I think the circumstances of our marriage are our affair. I would have thought you'd be pleased as Blair says he's going to leave you in the apartment.'

'I *am* pleased about that, but not to the extent that I want to see him sacrifice himself for some streetwise woman who has taken his fancy.'

Anger was surfacing now. It was bad enough, her father passing judgement on her, but now it was the turn of Blair's nearest and dearest to say their piece.

'You're very insulting,' she said, hiding her distress. 'Have you said all this to Blair?'

'Yes.'

'I see. And what did he say?'

'Not a lot. But, then, he wouldn't. He prefers to keep his affairs to himself. Though as the wedding is going to be soon, I suppose he thought it best to tell me the full story.'

Not exactly the full story, she thought. The last thing Blair would want would be for anyone to know that he was marrying her to protect her. Her brother-in-law-to-be wouldn't be surmising if he'd told him that. But he was dangerously close to the truth.

'I'm afraid you'll have to excuse me,' she told him. 'It would be better if you made any comments that you might have to Blair. And I think that Lauren would like a word with you before you leave. Why don't you keep out of my affairs and see to your own?'

'Huh?' he questioned, finding himself neatly side-tracked, but Imogen had gone, closing the door of her consulting room behind her with a decisive click.

Blair had been closeted with a salesman from one of the big pharmaceutical companies while this had been going on, and when he surfaced he said, 'Did I hear Simon's voice earlier?'

'Yes,' Imogen told him, raking her dark mop with an agitated hand. 'He came in to give me the third degree. He's not far off guessing the truth, Blair. Your brother thinks that if the baby is yours I'm guilty of entrapment, and if it isn't I have a cheek foisting it off on you. Either way, I suppose he has justification for not being too keen about what we're planning.'

'Forget about Simon,' he said calmly. 'It's usually me looking out for him. It will do him no harm to think about someone other than himself for once. And now, about that ring.'

'You're intending going ahead with it, then, in spite of what Simon said?'

'He'll calm down once he's adjusted. Earlier this

morning I told the staff here that we're going to be married and I meant it. You heard me, didn't you?'

'Yes, I heard you.'

'So we'll meet up when we've finished our calls and visit the nearest jeweller's.'

'Does it matter about a ring when it's all a sham?' she asked flatly.

'Even if *I* didn't think it necessary, your father would expect it,' he said blandly. 'So let's consider it settled.'

'Yes, but—' she protested.

He placed a finger on her lips. 'Stop making difficulties, Imogen. Start rehearsing the role of the happy bride-to-be.'

CHAPTER FIVE

ACT the happy bride-to-be, Imogen thought dismally as she turned away. She'd never been less happy about anything in her life. If Blair had asked her to marry him because they were madly in love, she would have been walking on air. But it was far from that.

He'd described it as a marriage of convenience, and she had to admit it would be very convenient for her. A protective husband and a father for her child as part of the package, as well as a comfortable lifestyle as Blair's wife.

But it would only be comfortable in a material sense. For the rest of it she would feel far from easy, knowing the circumstances that had brought it about.

What was he going to gain from it? she wondered. On the face of it...nothing. She'd been in his arms twice in recent days. The first time melting at his touch, aching for him to make love to her, but too guilt-ridden to let it proceed. And on the second occasion, what had she been like then? Sobbing out her misery.

Were either or both of those incidents connected with his sudden willingness to marry her? She doubted it. After the first time he'd held her he'd backed off as if he'd been burnt when she'd told him what was going on in her life, even though the next morning he'd had a change of heart. So why was he doing this?

She was the first to arrive at the jeweller's they'd chosen in the main shopping area of the city, and as she waited outside the shop Imogen was even more acutely aware that under normal circumstances this would be a happy occasion. A man and woman in love, picking out a ring that would tell the world they'd chosen to spend the rest of their lives together.

But in their case it was a farce, and the more she thought about it the more she knew she couldn't go through with it. They had ended up in this situation because of her father's intimidating ways and Blair's misguided concern.

He'd said that she needed looking after and she'd let him take over. But where had her independence gone? She was used to fending for herself. Had she fallen in with his plans because she wanted the man himself, on any terms?

Her face warmed as she admitted to herself there was something in that, but how could she be contemplating entering into something so important in so casual a manner?

And in the matter of her father, she'd faced up to him before on many things and she would do it again. He would have to be told the truth, and if he didn't like it…

At that moment she saw Blair striding towards her through the lunchtime crowds and he was something to see. Head and shoulders above most of them, with cool purpose in the deep brown eyes that went so oddly with the fair pelt of his hair, the sight of him was making her blood warm, but it wasn't wiping out her uncertainties.

Some people would say she was a fool, turning down the kind of life that Blair could give her. But a big house in the suburbs and a handsome husband would be heaven-sent only if there was love between them, instead of a fatherless baby.

'So,' he said with a smile for the sombre figure waiting for him, 'what kind of stones do you like? Something warm and fiery like you, maybe. I feel that diamonds are cold stones. How about rubies or emeralds?'

Imogen shook her head. He was making it even harder than she'd expected.

'I've changed my mind,' she said awkwardly. 'I can't go through with it, Blair. I know what you're trying to do and I bless you for it, but I've got myself into this mess and it's up to me to face up to it.'

As his face tightened with disbelief she went on, 'I'm going to tell my father the truth. I've never lied to him before and I'm not going to start now. Whatever he thinks of me, at least it will improve *your* standing with him when he hears what I have to say as he wasn't all that impressed when he thought you'd made me pregnant.'

'I don't care a damn what the old tyrant thinks of me,' he said abruptly. 'So that's it, then. The shortest engagement ever. Well, there's one person who will be pleased. Simon wasn't too happy about it from the start.'

'I'm not bothered about Simon,' she said quickly. 'How do *you* feel about it?'

He shrugged. 'Does it matter? But you'd better come up with a convincing story for the staff at the practice when we get back. Like I said, it must have been the shortest engagement on record.'

'I'll tell them that we've decided to wait until the baby's born before doing anything about getting married.'

'Tell them what you like,' he said in the same brusque tone. 'But don't expect me to go with you the next time you visit your father. And now, as I have some unexpected time on my hands, I'm going to do a home visit to the widow of an old friend who seems to be going down with something or other. I'll see you back at the practice.'

After coping with the astonishment of Lauren and the rest of them at the sudden change of plans, Imogen settled down to face the late afternoon surgery, having decided that once it was over she was going to visit her father, this time unannounced.

She'd heard Blair come back from the home visit that he'd mentioned and had kept out of his way. She sensed that he wasn't pleased at the way she'd backed out of the engagement and wasn't sure why.

He probably thought it was in keeping with her lack of common sense, she thought wryly. But surely he must be relieved to some degree. It had been on impulse that he'd offered to marry her and now she'd let him off the hook.

Her own feelings she was keeping bottled up. Time to bring them out into the open when she was alone in the privacy of her own place. And as the first patient of the afternoon came into her consulting room, she tuned in to someone else's needs instead of her own.

Michael Sullivan was a retired solicitor. Extremely fit for his age, he led an active social life and his records showed that it had been years since he'd consulted his GP. But today he was seating himself opposite and telling her, 'One of my eyelids keeps drooping, and apart from the fact that it's very irritating I would like to know the reason.'

When Imogen went round to the other side of the desk and examined his eye with an ophthalmoscope there was no sign of anything amiss, but it was a fact that patients suffering from ptosis, the medical term for drooping of the eyelid, could be at risk of a brain tumour or cerebral aneurysm, so it was up to their GP to have those possibilities checked out.

'You've not had a blow to the eye or any other kind of injury to that part of your face?' she questioned.

He shook his head.

'No. Nothing like that. It just came from nowhere.'

'This kind of thing does sometimes happen for no obvious reason,' she told him. 'But to be on the safe side I'm going to send you for a brain scan.'

'Good,' he said briskly. 'I'm not the sort of man to waste time in any area of my life, and if there is something amiss I want to know.'

Imogen smiled.

'That's good. You'd be surprised how many patients don't want to know.'

He was eyeing her appreciatively.

'How long have you been with the practice?'

'A matter of weeks. I was with a practice in the Midlands before.'

'I see. Well, nice to have met you, Dr Rossiter,' he said. 'Although I would have preferred it to be under happier circumstances.'

He got to his feet and, still observing her keenly, said, 'Rossiter. The name's familiar. Not related to Brian Rossiter, the chief constable, are you?'

Here we go again, she thought glumly. Would she ever be allowed to forget it?

'He's my father.'

'Well, I never! Stalwart chap. A force to be reckoned with…which is what the county needs.'

'Yes. I'm sure it is,' she agreed stiffly, with the

thought of the 'force' in question saying his piece that evening when he heard what she had to say.

Michael Sullivan was followed by two young women who'd come to arrange for the injections that would keep them safe while backpacking round the world.

They were of a similar age to herself, and she couldn't help thinking how different their lives were to her own. They were free and she was…what?

A mother-to-be, she told herself, and in spite of the complications that it brought with it her eyes sparkled at the thought.

But it was still all a long way off. Before anything else she had to talk to Blair, find out how he really felt about her decision not to marry him, while at the same time not letting him see how hard it had been to call off the wedding.

And when she'd done that and had told her father the truth, hopefully she would be able to put her mind to just two things—her pregnancy and the job.

'So you're still determined to tell your father that the wedding's off,' Blair said as they met briefly on the practice forecourt at the end of the day.

Imogen nodded.

'Yes, I'm going there now. And, Blair…?'

'What?'

'Can we talk?'

'What about?'

'Us.'

'Us!' he exclaimed. 'There isn't an us, Imogen. I know what was in your mind when you said you couldn't go through with the wedding. You want to prove that you can go it alone, don't you? Well, that's fine by me. I was merely trying to help.'

'What? By marrying someone who doesn't love you?'

It wasn't until she'd actually said it that she realised just how untrue it was. She did love him, had from the moment they'd met, and at another time, another place she would be telling him so.

She wanted to bite back the words, but what was the point? They weren't going anywhere together…and in any case it took two to make a loving partnership. If he'd been attracted to her before, he wasn't now.

Blair's face had whitened, whether with pain or anger she wasn't sure, but his reply when it came made her think that anger was the uppermost emotion.

'You seem to spread it around easily enough. Maybe I didn't see it as a problem,' he said through gritted teeth, and, leaving her to ponder on that, he got in his car and drove off.

Spread what around? she thought furiously as she drove the short distance to her father's house. Had Blair been inferring that he had her labelled as someone who'd become pregnant because she slept around?

She'd never told him the full story of Sean and herself so could she blame him if he did? But it hurt, even so.

When Blair arrived home Simon was at the restaurant so he wasn't able to tell him that the wedding was off. His smile was tight around the edges as he thought about how his younger brother had warned Imogen off.

He was going to find out that he needn't have bothered. Imogen had a mind of her own. Her agreement to the marriage had been a momentary blip and now her natural resilience was surfacing again. His offer to marry her had bounced back on him, and he was surprised at the degree of irritation and disappointment it was causing him.

He'd made the gesture in spontaneous concern for her and had meant it, without looking too deeply into his heart, and now he was back in the role of onlooker in her life.

As he cooked his evening meal her face was before him—the high cheek-bones, smooth ivory skin and the determined mouth. How was she coping with her father's response to her pregnancy? he wondered.

No doubt he would find out soon enough...if she was still speaking to him after his comment regarding her lifestyle. He'd no right to have said what he had. It had been said in pique and frustration. Instead of the relief that any sane man would have felt at being saved from making a fool of himself.

'I might have known!' Brian Rossiter said coldly when Imogen had finished saying her piece. 'Blair Nesbitt is not the type of man to make a woman pregnant outside marriage. He must be out of his mind, offering to take on someone who's having another man's child. And where is he, this fellow who's made you pregnant? Skulking in the background somewhere?'

'He's dead,' she said tonelessly.

Bushy grey brows shot up like a rocket. 'How? Where?' he rasped.

'He died in bad weather on Everest, along with a friend of his.'

'So he went doing something completely foolhardy when he'd given you a child.'

Imogen sighed.

The interrogation wasn't turning out as badly as she'd been expecting, but it was bad enough. She'd been hoping that Celia would be there to calm her father down, but she'd gone to some charity function and wouldn't be back until late.

'Sean didn't know I was pregnant when he went.'

'I see,' he said heavily, and she knew that the worst was over. 'So what about you and Blair Nesbitt?'

'It was just a gesture on his part,' she told him with eyes downcast. 'I wasn't thinking straight when I let him take responsibility for a problem that wasn't his. I've sorted it. There won't be a wedding.'

When she looked up she was amazed to see that her father was actually smiling.

'Spoken like a true Rossiter,' he said. 'We don't always see eye to eye but you're not short of courage, Imogen. And in any case, lies don't get anyone anywhere.'

She let out a deep breath. What a pity Blair wasn't here to hear this, she thought. He would know that she'd done the right thing in refusing to marry him. Yet there was little satisfaction in the thought because she knew deep down that she had wanted to marry him…more than anything else on earth.

On the way home Imogen called at Blair's apartment. She'd never been there before and under other circumstances would have been curious to see inside, but tonight her mind was full of many things and the decor of Blair's place wasn't one of them.

'Imogen,' he said without surprise when he opened the door to her. 'Come in.'

'I've called to tell you what happened with my dad,' she said quickly, anxious to explain her presence.

'Yes. I thought you might have,' he said quietly,

pointing to the sofa. 'Take a seat. Can I get you a drink?'

'No, thanks,' she told him with the feeling that she wasn't exactly as welcome as the buds in spring. 'Dad was a bit grim at first, but he was pleased that I'd been honest with him and I think even more pleased that his opinion of you hadn't been tarnished.'

'And what's his opinion of you?'

She grimaced.

'Something like yours, only more so.'

'And what's that supposed to mean?'

'That you think I'm a bit stupid. What was it you described me as? Someone who spreads my affections around easily enough.'

'Yes, well, I apologise. That was said in anger. You are the only one who knows if it's true.'

Her face crumpled but she fought back the tears. No way was she going to weep in front of him again, but she had to ask, 'Why are you so angry with me, Blair? I thought you'd be glad that you'd been saved the kind of marriage that ours would have been.'

His jaw tightened. 'It's myself I'm angry with, not you. Goodness knows, you've had enough to put up with in recent months without being the recipient of my bad humour. It's just that I don't like untidy arrangements. I prefer my life to be organised and you have to admit that isn't easy when you're around.'

Imogen found herself smiling through her tears.

'I'm not sure if that is meant to be critical or complimentary, but I could make a guess. And now I'm going, Blair. It's been a long day... And thanks for being there for me when I needed you.'

On impulse she put her arms around him and gave him a hug, and as if the gesture had switched on an electric current he returned the embrace, but there was nothing casual about the way he was holding her.

It was like that night in her apartment in the seconds before she'd told him about her pregnancy. The age-old chemistry between the sexes. And for a brief enchanted moment Imogen put the thought of the baby to the back of her mind and pretended that there were no obstacles to separate her from this man she'd fallen in love with.

He groaned and his arms fell away.

'You need to make up your mind, Imogen,' he told her. 'If you're going to start dangling your sexuality in front of me like a carrot, I might just decide to take a bite.'

'I wasn't dangling anything,' she protested angrily. 'I was merely trying to say thank you, but I'll make sure it doesn't happen again. Goodnight, Blair.'

When Imogen had gone Blair went to the window and watched her go to her car. The lithe slenderness of her was already thickening, he thought morosely. That fact alone should have told him to have more sense than let himself be aroused by her nearness.

And now she'd gone home miserable and confused, but not any more confused than he was. One second he was telling himself that his feelings for her were the concern that he would feel for any woman in her position, and the next he was having to admit there was more to it than that…much more.

Why couldn't his yearnings be directed at someone less complicated than Imogen? He'd invited her to join the practice and had had no cause for regrets on that score, but it was the rest of it that was driving him crazy.

He was charmed by her vibrancy. The dark allure of

her. The way she stood up to her father. And he envied the poor dead guy who'd given her a child.

During the weeks that followed a calmer atmosphere prevailed between them. With the spectre of her father's anger out of the way and on the face of it Blair back to his usual crisp and pleasant self. Imogen was beginning to settle into her pregnancy with a more tranquil mind.

If any of the staff thought it strange that she and Blair spent no time together out of surgery hours no one commented, and if she spent the warm summer evenings in pensive solitude no one but her knew it.

There was a park near her apartment and sometimes she went to sit there, now a bulky figure in a loose top and stretch jeans.

She watched parents with young children feeding the ducks or sailing toy boats on a small lake. Lovers wandering hand in hand along tree-lined paths. And she envied them their togetherness.

One night in late July the park's leisurely appeal was missing. Those who were there looked nervous and apprehensive, and officers from two police cars parked near a secluded wooded area mostly frequented by courting couples were cordoning it off and preparing to erect a tent.

Imogen could see a slender leg, shoeless and bloodstained, sticking out of the bushes and her heartbeat quickened. Something was very much amiss.

There was a gathering of the curious nearby and a police officer was asking them to move away, but there was no immediate response and he had to repeat the request more demandingly.

The general public with its morbid fascination for

crime and its accompanying gruesome details wasn't going to miss out on some excitement, and they were still showing a reluctance to depart.

Imogen stepped forward and received a hard stare from the officer.

'I'm Dr Imogen Rossiter, and I'm a police surgeon,' she told him. 'I was out for a stroll and saw that there'd been some sort of incident. Can I be of any help?'

His face lightening, he lifted the tape and beckoned her forward.

'Possibly. We have a suspicious death. One of the park attendants found the body of a young woman in the bushes. Someone like you has just arrived but you can come through if you want to.'

The eyes of the girl lying in the stillness of death stared up at Blair lifelessly as he bent over her. Anger rose in him. She was just a kid. Sixteen or seventeen maybe. Well-dressed and cared for, she was somebody's cherished child and her life had been snuffed out.

A footstep behind had him turning and he threw Imogen a grim smile when he saw her standing there. 'Where have you sprung from?' he asked, turning back to the body.

'I was passing and saw the commotion,' she told him, dropping to her knees beside him. 'What gives?'

He pointed to thumbprints on the neck and the face that had turned a bluish shade of purple from congested blood.

'All the signs of strangulation. It wouldn't take long with a pair of strong hands. There's nothing to indicate that a ligature was used.'

'Poor child,' she said sombrely.

'Yes, indeed,' he agreed. 'It doesn't matter how

many deaths of this kind we see, it never gets to be any less painful.'

'Any sexual interference?'

'Not visibly. There are no semen stains on the clothing but that's a job for the pathology people.'

At that moment there was a shout from officers searching the undergrowth further along the path.

'Sarge!' a young constable bellowed. 'We've found another body.'

The two police surgeons eyed each other in surprise.

'This I don't believe,' Blair said as they joined those hurrying towards where the shout had come from.

It was a youth this time, of a similar age to the girl and badly battered around the head.

'There must be a lunatic around this place!' Blair said in cold rage as they knelt beside him. 'First the girl and now this young fellow.'

'Aye,' the police sergeant said. 'Somebody has given him a real going over. How long would you say they've both been dead?'

'What do you think?' Blair asked of her.

'The body temperatures indicate a space of a few hours,' she replied. 'Rigor mortis is only just beginning to set in.'

He nodded his agreement.

'Yes. I'd say they were killed within a short time of each other. In what order it would be hard to say.'

The crowd was pressing forward again, their excitement at fever pitch with the finding of a second corpse, and when Imogen looked up she saw that she was being watched.

The man was standing on his own beneath a clump of trees, an unkempt-looking fellow with long greasy hair and furtive eyes. She shuddered.

Blair saw it and asked, 'What's wrong?'

'Nothing,' she said firmly.

Just because some down and out had given her a second glance, it didn't mean that he was a villain.

'Are you sure?' he persisted.

'Yes, I'm sure.'

When Imogen looked across again the man had gone and she breathed a sigh of relief. He was probably only watching out of interest like the rest of the crowd, but she did wonder if the police had noticed him as they seemed to be more intent on grilling the unfortunate park attendant than spreading themselves around.

After they'd finished examining the two bodies and Blair had recorded his findings on tape for the pathologist, they packed up their equipment and prepared to leave the police to their enquiries.

'I'll drive you home,' he said, 'but I'll have to get a move on as I'm taking someone out for a meal.'

'There's no need. My place is only five minutes' walk away,' she said immediately, miffed that someone else, probably a woman, was going to have Blair's company for the rest of the evening.

With a casual wave of the hand Imogen pointed herself in the direction of her apartment, leaving him with no chance to say anything further.

She had barely had time to lock the door behind her when the doorbell rang and she found herself smiling. Was it his turn to be peeved because she'd left him so abruptly? Or had he changed his mind and decided that it was *her* company he wanted?

That wasn't likely, though, was it? In recent weeks there'd been countless times when he could have sought her out in the evenings or at weekends, but her doorbell and phone had been silent.

So sure that it was Blair, she didn't look through the peep-hole in the door, and as it swung back with a vicious swish she knew she'd done a very foolish thing.

Her hands came out to slam it shut but she wasn't quick enough. The man who'd been in the park rammed it back with his foot and then he was in the hallway of the apartment with his hands around her throat.

She couldn't cry out or even move. It was as if he had her neck in a vice and all she could think about was how long would her baby live after she was dead? Would they find her body in time to save it?

'I saw you looking down your nose at me back there in the park,' he snarled. 'All pretty, pretty, working for the police. You weren't clever enough to know I was following you, though, were you?

'You're just like those two kids. Full of your own importance. The girl laughed at me when I tried to talk to her. Said she was waiting for her boyfriend and that I needed a bath. She wasn't laughing when I'd finished with her, though, and neither was he when he showed up. Never saw what hit him.'

His voice seemed to be coming from a long way off and she thought weakly that this was how it must be when death was near. A gradual withdrawing from life into the unknown.

But help was at hand. Someone else had hurled himself through the open door and her attacker was gripped from behind with a force that made him loosen his hold on her throat.

As she slumped against the wall, gasping for breath, she saw Blair and the intruder struggling in the door-way. Picking up a vase from the hall table, she staggered up to them and hit the fellow on the head. As she watched in a dazed sort of surprise, Blair followed it up with a blow to the jaw and the man caved in at the knees and sank to the floor.

'Well done,' Blair gasped with his foot on the murderer's chest. 'Can you manage to phone the police before this madman comes round, Imogen?'

She nodded and, after croaking the necessary details of the attack and impressing on the person at the other end of the line that they had the murderer in the apartment, she lowered herself onto the nearest chair.

Blair's eyes were glowing like hot brown coals from the fury inside him as he'd listened to what she'd said. Imogen had told the police that this fellow was the murderer, he thought incredulously, and the only way she could know that was because he'd admitted it.

He'd seen the man in the park but hadn't taken much notice of him until he'd seen him following Imogen as he'd been about to pull away from where he'd parked his car and alarm bells had started to ring.

When he'd decided to keep tabs on him, the engine had refused to start, and after fiddling with it for precious minutes he'd hurried round to her apartment on foot. And, he thought raggedly, he'd only just got there in time.

If anything had happened to his Imogen, he would have gone insane, he told himself, and didn't even notice that he'd thought of her as his.

She was crouching there, white and shaken, and he wanted to take her in his arms and hold her close, but there was no way he was going to move an inch from his captive until the police arrived.

When they came dashing in with truncheons at the ready, the attacker was beginning to come round. Yanking him to his feet, Blair told them, 'Dr Rossiter is very shaken up, and I want to examine her as soon as possible, but I think she has something to tell you about the murders first, as she was nearly victim number three.'

While they were taking the man to the police van outside, one of the officers took from Imogen the details of what had happened. When she'd finished he closed his notebook with a satisfied snap and said, 'So he'll be facing two murder charges and an attempted. We'll need you to come down to the station to make a full statement as soon as you feel up to it, Dr Rossiter.' He turned to Blair who was hovering anxiously. 'The lady is all yours, sir.'

He wished she was, Blair thought as he examined her neck with gentle hands. If he'd arrived at the apartment any later, he could have lost her.

The brutal finger marks were there as a sombre reminder of her ordeal and Imogen's voice was hoarse and strained, but her larynx and vocal cords seemed to be uninjured.

When he'd finished checking her over, he said soberly, 'I should never have let you get involved with what was my call-out. I think that you should drop the police surgeon work for the next few months as we both know that it brings us into touch with some seedy characters.'

Imogen didn't answer but he sensed that she wouldn't easily agree to that suggestion so, changing the subject, he asked, 'Was it something to do with that man when you were shuddering in the park?'

'Yes,' she admitted. 'I felt as if he was watching me.'

'And so why didn't you say so when I asked you what was wrong?'

'I don't know. I thought I might be imagining it.'

'Well, you weren't imagining what came afterwards, were you?'

'No, I wasn't,' she said bleakly. 'I was sure it was you at the door when I opened it. So sure that I didn't check first. I could have paid for it with my life if you hadn't arrived.'

'I saw him following you and decided that I'd better keep an eye on him.'

'So you weren't coming here in any case?'

'Well, no. I said I had an appointment if you remember.'

So much for her conceit, she thought. But did it matter? He had been there when she'd needed him and that was the important thing.

But Blair always seemed to be there when she needed him, and yet what had she ever done for him? Nothing. Except cause him aggravation. He must see her as a perpetual millstone around his neck.

He was watching the changing expressions on Imogen's face and said gently, 'Go on. Let's hear it.'

'Hear what?'

'Something is going on in your head. I can tell.'

'I'm thinking that I'm always causing you grief.'

He laughed.

'Yes, you are. My life was peaceful before you came along.'

'And is that how you want it to be again?'

'Not necessarily.'

'I *am* trying to keep out of your way.'

'And I out of yours,' he said in the same even tone. 'Though it's as if that isn't meant to be. But enough of theorising. You've just come through a dreadful ordeal and I'm taking you back to my place for the night.

I know that crazy man is in custody but I want to keep an eye on you…and the baby.'

'But you haven't got room,' she protested.

'No problem. I'll sleep on the couch.' Taking her arm, he led her out into the hallway and informed a couple of curious neighbours who were hovering, 'Dr Rossiter will be away for the night.'

CHAPTER SIX

BLAIR awoke in the early hours and found Simon standing by the couch.

'What's Imogen Rossiter doing, sleeping in your bed?' he asked curiously, and Blair gave a wintry smile.

'Well, she's certainly not Goldilocks with that dark mop. We've had quite a night. I thought you might have heard what happened in the park earlier.'

Simon shook his head.

'No. What?'

'Two teenagers were found murdered. I was called out to the first one and the second corpse was discovered while I was there. Imogen was passing by and stopped to assist. Incredibly the fellow who'd killed the youngsters was still loitering and he followed her home and attacked her, too.

'I got there in the nick of time and now that's where he is…in the nick. Imogen was shaken up, as you can imagine, and I brought her back here so that I could keep an eye on her.'

Simon whistled softly.

'Gee! All that's been happening while I've been standing over a hot stove!'

Their voices had aroused Imogen from a fitful sleep and the moment she surfaced the soreness of her neck and throat were there to remind her that not so long ago she'd thought she was going to die.

As she padded downstairs to the kitchen to find herself a drink, the baby inside her moved and she became still. She wanted to go to Blair and place his hand on her stomach so that he could share in the magical moment. But, she asked herself achingly, would it mean anything to him if she did? After all, it wasn't his child inside there.

The next day was Saturday and it was Imogen's turn to take the short morning surgery that was forerunner to the weekend. But when she came down to breakfast Blair was already up and dressed.

When she eyed him questioningly he said, 'Needless to say, you won't be on duty at the practice today, Imogen. I'll do it and when I get back I'll run you home.

'And so how are you this morning?' he asked as she poured herself a coffee.

'Glad to be alive, which is more than those two poor youngsters can say.'

He nodded sombrely.

'Indeed. I can't get the picture of that fellow with his hands round your throat out of my mind. Thankfully he won't be seeing the outside of prison for a long time to come. If that were not the case I wouldn't have a moment's peace of mind every time you were out of my sight.'

Suddenly she was filled with a desperate longing to know just how deep his concern for her went and, without giving herself time to reconsider, she asked, 'Is that how you would feel about anyone who'd had that kind of experience? Or do I matter more?'

Huddled in one of his robes, with her hair tousled from sleep and her neck covered in bruises, it was hardly the moment for heart-searching or romantic dallying, but she had to ask.

Blair smiled, a teasing kind of smile that told her she wasn't going to get a satisfactory answer.

'You have to matter more, don't you?' he said easily. 'We're both doctors, both police surgeons. Wherever I go, whatever I do, I find myself entangled with you in some form or other. So, yes...I'd say that you do invade my consciousness more than most people.'

She glared at him.

'In other words, we're back to the nuisance factor, but you're trying to be polite about it.'

He was laughing now.

'If the cap fits, yes,' he said, and added as he turned to go, 'Simon won't be surfacing for hours. It was four a.m. when he came in. I've cooked you some breakfast. It's in the oven on a low setting. Make sure that you eat it. That child of yours needs looking after. It must be wondering what sort of a world it's coming into.'

'And what sort of a mother it's going to be saddled with?' she questioned defensively.

Blair wasn't laughing now. His face had a closed-up look.

'I don't think it need have any worries on that score,' he said abruptly, and made his departure.

The receptionist on duty at the Saturday morning surgery buttonholed him as soon as he walked in.

'The chief constable is waiting for you,' she said, pointing to his consulting room. 'I've settled him in there and made him a cup of tea.'

Blair nodded. He could make a guess what this was about—last night. He was right. Brian Rossiter got to his feet when he saw him and asked brusquely. 'Where is Imogen? I've been to her place but there's no sign of her. I know what happened in the park last night and back at her apartment, and I want to see for myself that she's all right.'

'I took her home with me for the night,' Blair told him. 'She was very shaken up and I was concerned for her and the baby. Her throat is bruised and sore and her voice rather croaky, but apart from that she seems all right. Needless to say, I'll be keeping a close watch on her.'

Brian sighed.

'You'll be a better man than I am if you can do that. So what's your address? I'll go round there as I won't be happy until I've seen her for myself.' The older man held Blair's gaze. 'I could have lost my daughter and my grandchild if you hadn't got there in time. It's a sobering thought.

'Imogen is fortunate to have you looking out for her and just between the two of us, I would have been damned glad if you *had* been the father of this child of hers. I don't know what your feelings are on the matter, but you must have some or you wouldn't have been ready to stand in for the other fellow.'

Just as Blair was beginning to think that maybe the old tartar wasn't so bad after all, Brian reverted back to form.

'But I hope you're aware that though that daughter of mine is a pretty young filly, she needs to be kept on a firm rein or she'll kick over the traces.'

'So Imogen's not a chip off the old block, then?' Blair asked blandly.

For a moment Brian looked taken aback and then, clearing his throat, said. 'Er…no. Certainly not.' As if he'd said enough on that subject, he went on to inform

Blair, 'Someone from the division will be coming round to question her and take a statement. But I've given instructions that they don't approach her until I give permission.'

They could hear voices in the waiting room and, taking it as his cue to leave, the chief constable bade Blair a brief farewell and went to seek out his daughter.

Emily Bradshaw was an elderly lady who came to consult Blair periodically about the aches and pains of old age. She also had diabetes, which he and the practice nurses kept a close watch on. Today she had presented herself at the surgery because of a scare with her eyes the previous night.

'I suppose it's the optician I should be talking to,' she said, puffing heavily as she seated herself opposite him, 'but mine has just changed hands and I'd rather see somebody who knows about my complaints.'

'So what's the problem, Emily?' he asked when she'd got her breath back.

'It was last night, Doctor. I was in the garden, chatting to my neighbour, when I got this flashing yellow light in front of my right eye. At first I thought it was an insect buzzing about in front of me and then I realised it was my eye. Something had happened to it. I didn't sleep all night for wondering if it was the retina that had slipped. That happened to my brother and because he didn't get it seen to right away he lost the sight of the eye.'

She was in her late eighties but he thought there was nothing wrong with her thinking processes. It could very well be that it was the retina at risk, but an optician would have been the best person to consult because they were better equipped for that sort of thing.

His ophthalmoscope showed little out of the ordinary when he examined the eye but, aware that people with her condition could be subject to vitreous haemorrhages due to diabetic retinopathy, he felt that she should see an ophthalmic consultant with all haste.

The condition arose from the forming of new fragile blood capillaries attaching themselves to the retina. Inclined to bleed easily, they would temporarily affect vision, but in most cases the vitreous haemorrhage that they'd caused would be reabsorbed and the transparent eye gel restored. But, and it was an important 'but', there was always the possibility that the retina might have become detached due to the impact of the haemorrhage.

'I'm going to arrange for an ambulance to take you to hospital, Emily,' he told her. 'I know that it's the weekend but they do have an eye clinic on Saturday mornings. There are a few things that it could be and they're not so serious as a detached retina, but we have to be on the safe side. So just sit tight and I'll ask the receptionist to phone the emergency services.'

When he came back from organising the ambulance the old lady was looking apprehensive so he said soothingly, 'Now, don't worry. They'll take good care of you and will take you back home afterwards.'

'It's not that I'm worried about,' she told him. 'I've left a casserole in the oven.'

Blair hid a smile. Running true to type, her anxieties had switched from retina to casserole.

'Can we ring your neighbour and ask her to keep an eye on it for you?' he suggested.

Emily shook her head.

'No. We don't get on. It will be done by twelve o'clock and by the time I get back from the hospital it will be all dried up. I know what those places are like. I could be there for hours. They might even keep me in.'

'Where do you keep a spare key?'

'Under the plant pot by the back door.'

'Right. So I'll go and switch the oven off for you at twelve o'clock. I pass your place on my way home.'

Her face brightened.

'That's good of you, Doctor. And while you're there, the cat will want feeding. I'm expecting a parcel, too. I hope they won't have left it outside my front door... And the milkman calls for his money around lunchtime on a Saturday. If you see him, tell him I'll pay him on Monday.'

'I'll take the parcel inside if it's there, Emily,' he told her with the feeling that he'd just bitten off more than he could chew. 'And I'll keep an eye open for the milkman. Tell me, what does your cat have for his dinner?'

'It's a her,' she told him. 'Her name's Tabitha and there's milk in the fridge and a tin of cat food on the shelf.'

'And the tin-opener?'

'In the knife-and-fork drawer where you would expect it to be,' she said sharply, as if he were from another planet.

'Fine,' he said smoothly. 'Only sometimes things aren't always where we expect them to be, are they?'

'They are in my house. A place for everything and everything in its place.'

While the practice nurse and the receptionist were helping Emily into the ambulance, Blair was getting ready to finish for the day. He was anxious to get back to Imogen, even though she'd seemed all right when he'd left her.

The events of the night before had shaken him to the core. Yet who knew better than he that health problems and crime were two things that walked hand in hand with distress and danger. If he and Imogen had chosen to include the latter as part of their chosen careers, taking risks was going to be the name of the game.

There'd been just a smattering of patients in the waiting room when he'd arrived and apart from Emily most of them had been there for only minor ailments, but as he was on the point of leaving a mother came in with a young boy who was looking decidedly green around the gills.

'Lee has fallen off his skateboard and hurt his arm, Doctor,' she said anxiously. 'He's been vomiting on the way here. Says the pain is making him feel sick, and he almost fainted as we were getting out of the car.'

The lad was obviously in a lot of pain and as Blair examined his arm he said, 'Tell me how you fell, Lee.'

'I was coming down this ramp and lost control. I put my hand out to try and stop myself falling and landed on it,' he muttered awkwardly. 'I felt a pain in my elbow like a knife going in.'

Blair nodded and, turning to his mother, said, 'That's what I thought. Very often when a person, particularly a child, falls onto an outstretched hand it results in fractures of the lower end of the humerus, the upper arm bone where it joins the elbow.'

'Fractures! More than one?' she questioned.

'It's possible, but only an X-ray will tell us that. You're going to have to take Lee to Accident and

Emergency, I'm afraid. The vomiting and faintness are due to the pain and shock. Keep him warm and quiet, without anything to eat or drink until you get there, in case they have to operate.'

With a smile for the boy he said, 'You've no idea how many lads of your age break their bones from skateboarding, but I suppose it's no use suggesting that you give it up.'

As Lee shook his head his mother said grimly, 'We'll have to see what your father says about that, young man. But we've more important things to worry about at the moment. Let's get you to hospital.'

When they'd gone Blair said to the nurse and receptionist who'd been assisting, 'Let's go before anyone else collars us.' As they had no objections to that, within minutes he was locking the outer door and pointing himself towards home, calculating that he would have just enough time to collect Imogen before going to do the chores at Emily's house.

'I feel a fraud, sitting around here while you're doing all the work,' Imogen said when he got back.

Blair smiled. She'd been on his mind since the moment of leaving the house, even though he'd known she was safe enough at his place.

'Don't worry about that,' he told her. 'Has your father been to see you? He was waiting at the surgery when I got there, all steamed up and anxious because he'd been to your apartment and you weren't there.'

'Yes, he's been,' she said wryly. 'He said that I should have let you marry me when you wanted to. That you would have kept me out of mischief. He was just like he always is. As soon as he'd satisfied himself I was all in one piece, it was back to the old gripes.'

'As to me keeping you out of mischief, last night's affair was a lot more than that,' Blair told her. 'I wouldn't like to think of you in that kind of danger ever again. So, as I've already suggested, I think that for the time being you should opt out of police surgeon activities.'

'I'm doing no such thing!' she protested. 'Last night was a one-off and I'm tired of being told what to do. First my dad and then you.'

She'd told him what her father had said about their proposed marriage because she was desperate to know whether he regretted it or was relieved that it hadn't taken place. But it seemed that he had no comment to make and, short of asking him outright, it looked as if she wasn't going to get to know his feelings on the matter.

Her own were crystal clear. She wanted Blair in her life more than she'd ever wanted anything. But not as a substitute husband or father. She wanted him loving her, lusting for her. But the first move had to come from him as she was the one with the baggage...the unborn child curled beneath her ribs.

And that was the crux of the matter, wasn't it? She was pregnant with someone else's child, for heaven's sake. What was he supposed to do?

Though maybe he'd already done it. Stepped back. Taken the opportunity she'd given him to escape from the crazy marriage they'd been contemplating. And the more he kept his distance, the more she ached for him.

But he was here now. Observing her thoughtfully with the eyes that seemed to know what was in her mind before she even knew herself.

'All right,' he said levelly. 'There's no need to start flaunting your independence at those who are concerned for you. Your father cares for you in his own crusty way and I...'

He paused and she interrupted frostily, 'You were saying? I can't stand it when people stop in the middle of a sentence.'

'All right! All right! *I* also feel a certain amount of responsibility for you.'

'And why would that be?'

'Because you are part of the practice for one thing and I owe it to the rest of those working there that you should be happy and healthy for their sakes...your sake...and for your child's sake.'

'Is that it?' she asked dolefully.

Blair took a step towards her and her heartbeat quickened.

'You know it isn't. You are the most enchanting woman I've ever met.'

They were only inches apart. Imogen could see an unmistakable purpose in the dark eyes beneath his short golden crop and she caught her breath. She needed his arms around her like she needed to breathe.

Yet now it seemed as if he was rooted to the spot as he went on to say flatly, 'But the pattern of your life was mapped out before we met. Surely you realise that. I mistakenly tried to step in and offer some support, but you wisely saw further ahead than I and called the wedding off. So what do you want me to say, Imogen?'

'Nothing,' she said with a careless shrug. 'Nothing at all.'

'Right. So if you're ready I'll take you home...and on the way I have to call and turn Emily Bradshaw's oven off, feed her cat, deal with the milkman if he's around and bring in the mail.'

'So every cloud has a silver lining for some,' she
said, laughter wiping away the doldrums. 'With old
Mrs Bradshaw being at the top of the list. How did you
get involved in her affairs to such an extent?'

He smiled back at her as if their frustrating discussion had never taken place.

'It's a long story. I'll tell you another time, but now
we must get going or Emily will never forgive me if
her casserole is spoiled.'

When they arrived at Imogen's apartment Blair
watched her expression. He'd decided that if she
showed any fear at returning to the scene of the previous night's attack he was going to take her back to
his place until she found somewhere else to live.

He needn't have worried. She looked sombre but not
afraid as she looked around her. Everywhere was much
as they'd left it. A broken ornament on the floor and a
lamp overturned were soon dealt with, and as the intruder had got no further than the hall the rest of the
place was how it had been before he'd burst in.

Imogen knew Blair was watching her and she told
him, 'I'll be fine, Blair. After all, the fellow is locked
up and he won't be getting bail after what he's done.
It was lucky for me that he didn't know who my father
is or he really would have been out to get me. As it
was, he came after me because he said I was a "pretty,
pretty" working for the police, which I suppose means
that he thought I was looking down at him.

'The girl in the park had already made him feel in-
adequate once and then I turned up, seven months pregnant and helping to run the show for the police.'

'If that's the case, why didn't he go after me?' Blair
questioned. 'I was in charge.'

'Because you're not pregnant and ''pretty, pretty'' like me.'

'You're certainly that,' he said quietly.

'Pregnant? Yes. There's no getting away from that.'

'I meant pretty.'

'What, even with the bump?' she questioned laughingly.

'Yes, even with the bump. Until last night's affair you were positively glowing.'

'I was?'

'Oh, for goodness' sake, Imogen. Don't you ever look in the mirror?'

'Yes, I do!' she cried. 'And what do you think I see?'

'I don't know, but I have a feeling that you're going to tell me.'

'I see a full-breasted vision with extended waistline and swollen feet.'

'Oh, dear! You do want this baby, don't you?'

She smiled.

'Yes, of course I do. I can't wait to hold it in my arms. It's just that I do so wish…'

'What? What do you wish?' he asked softly.

Imogen turned away. She wished that the child inside her was his. That was what she wished. But a rebuff would put out her light for evermore.

Blair took her arm and swivelled her round to face him again, and this time he wasn't reading her mind.

'You're wishing that the waiting was over, aren't you?'

'Yes. That's it,' she fibbed, hoping that she sounded convincing.

He reached out and touched her cheek with gentle fingers. 'I know it's hard for you, having to face this alone with the baby's father gone, but at least you've got your father, who seems to be mellowing to some degree, and that nice wife of his. And I'm here on the sidelines ready to help in any way that I can.'

That's just it, she wanted to tell him. I don't want you on the sidelines. I want you in the centre of my life.

But it was there again. The feeling that the scales weren't evenly balanced. When the baby came it would be two to one and Blair had never mentioned marriage since the day she'd told him she'd changed her mind.

Better get back to more positive thinking, she told herself, and dredged up a smile. 'Yes, I know that Dad and Celia will stand by me. She's offered to have the baby in the mornings for me so that I won't have to bring it to the practice or take it to a childminder, and I'll sort something out for the afternoons. You didn't know what you were letting yourself in for when you met me, did you?'

'I think I might have done, but I never could resist a challenge,' he told her drily.

It would be so easy to tell Imogen that from the moment of their meeting he'd wanted her in his life, and when he'd discovered that he couldn't have her in the way that he'd wanted her he'd been willing to accept what had been on offer so entranced had he been with her. And even now, with no binding ties of any kind between them, he still longed to feel the vibrant warmth of her in his arms.

But, he told himself, at least he was still around her. He'd been there for her last night, thank God, and with the memory of that came the reminder of what her father had said.

'The police will want to question you about last

night,' he said, causing her to blink at the sudden return to normality. 'But your father said they'd been told to wait until he gave permission.'

'Yes, he told me and I've assured him that any time they want to come I'm up to it. Have we heard anything else about the murders?'

'Not as yet. With taking morning surgery I haven't had much time to enquire and your father didn't come up with any details. But, no doubt, sooner or later all will be revealed.'

'That maniac told me that he'd tried to chat the girl up while she was waiting for her boyfriend and when she told him to go away and have a bath, he killed her and then lay in wait for the boyfriend. From the sound of it he attacked him from behind—in his own words, the poor kid didn't know what hit him.

'Sick object that he is, he stayed around after the bodies were found. I suppose it must have given him a buzz to see all the excitement that he had created and to watch the park attendant being interrogated. Then for some reason he zoomed in on me.'

'All of this must have happened in the late afternoon or early evening,' Blair said in incredulous anger. 'How could he have killed two people without being seen?'

'The devil was obviously looking after his own,' she said sombrely. 'That part of the park is more secluded than the rest. There are lots of mature trees and bushes and narrow paths that lead to seats that are out of sight. His kind snoop on courting couples and it would seem that it went a lot further than that with this fellow.'

'Indeed,' he agreed heavily. 'So keep the door locked when I've gone and promise me that you won't ever open it again without checking first.'

'Yes, of course. I was so sure that it was you there that for the first time ever I didn't look through the peep-hole.'

Because of wishful thinking, she could have told him, but didn't. Talking about those fraught moments reminded her that he'd arranged to meet someone and had never got there.

'What about the person you were intending dining with last night?' she asked.

'That was Briony Matthews. I've told you about her before. I rang later in the evening to tell her what had happened. I take her out occasionally. She needed a lot of support when her husband died and I felt that I ought to be there for her.'

'And how long ago was that?' she asked with a feeling that depression was looming.

'Nine months.'

'I recall Simon mentioning her. He seemed to think that she had you in line for husband number two.'

Blair shrugged.

'That brother of mine needs to sort out his own affairs before he starts interfering in mine. He's started dating Lauren at the practice and I'm sure he wouldn't like me to start passing comments about that.'

'So is this Briony person in love with you?'

She watched his mouth tighten.

'Does it matter?'

Yes, it does, Imogen wanted to shriek at him, but I can't admit it because I have no claim on you.

So instead she made do with, 'No, I suppose not. I was just curious.'

'I don't remember asking you about your private life,' he said unsmilingly. 'Such as how long had you been sleeping with your child's father? How serious was it? Would you have married him if he hadn't been killed?'

'No. You haven't asked me,' she agreed. 'Which made me think that you weren't interested. But if you want some answers, you can have them. I slept with Sean just the once. It wasn't a serious relationship and, no, I wouldn't have married him just for the child's sake.'

He was eyeing her incredulously. 'Yet you would have married me. Someone that you barely knew!'

'Yes,' she told him defiantly. 'What do you make of that?'

'I'm damned if I know. But in any case that's something else that doesn't matter. It's water under the bridge.'

'Yes, it is,' she agreed tonelessly.

'I'm going,' he said suddenly. 'You're still pale and shaken up from yesterday without all the soul-searching that we seem to be determined to inflict upon ourselves. Why not go to bed for a few hours, Imogen? I'll make you a snack first if you like and then tuck you up for the afternoon.'

'I'm not hungry, but I will go to bed. And, Blair, I know I'm beginning to sound like a gramophone record, but thanks again for always being around when I need you.' Reaching up, she pressed her lips to his cheek.

He became still and then in a voice that was suddenly hoarse said, 'So can I break all my firm resolutions and claim a reward for my good deeds?'

She nodded, eyes wide and waiting.

'Here goes, then,' he breathed. Cupping her face in his hands, he kissed her long and lingeringly. But even as she began to melt at his touch he was putting her

away from him and telling her quickly, 'Don't tempt
me any further. By the time I get home I will be regretting what I've just done.'

Imogen glowered at him. 'Thanks a bunch. In other
words, you just felt like a bit of dilly-dallying and the
local easy lay was available.'

'Don't be ridiculous, Imogen,' he told her, 'and will
you now, please, go and have that rest?'

'When will I see you again?' she asked pensively.

He was turning to go.

'I'll ring tomorrow.' And off he went, making sure
that the door was securely shut behind him.

CHAPTER SEVEN

THE antenatal clinic these days was a more relaxed affair than normally because the doctor in charge was an expectant mother herself, which made it easier for those attending to talk about their health problems and domestic worries.

It was generally accepted by staff and patients alike that the baby Imogen was carrying was Blair Nesbitt's in view of the marriage plans that had been put on hold until after the birth.

The only one who had questioned the baby's parentage at that time had been Simon and, as he had immediately lost interest once the wedding had been called off, Imogen had seen no need to enlighten anyone regarding the circumstances of her pregnancy.

It was mainly for Blair's sake, to save him embarrassment. And for her own part she saw no necessity to make public her past indiscretions, deciding that if no wedding materialised after the birth, interest in her affairs would have died down by then.

But, having been almost three months pregnant when she joined the practice, she and Blair were aware that they needed to give the impression that they'd been sleeping together before she'd started at the Sycamores, otherwise there would be a time discrepancy when the child was born.

'Do you know what sex your baby is?' one of the women attending the clinic asked the week after the murders in the park.

Imogen shook her head.

'No. I'd rather wait and see.'

'Mine's a girl,' she said despondently. 'I've already got four daughters and we desperately wanted a boy, so we decided we'd have one more try, but it hasn't worked.'

Imogen flashed the patient a sympathetic smile.

'I'm sure you'll love her just the same.'

The woman sighed. 'Yes, we will, but...'

'I know. It would have been nice to have a son.'

It was a day when everyone at the clinic seemed to have a problem and by the time it was over she was thinking that she was the fortunate one.

A twenty-five-year-old, a third of the way into her pregnancy, had turned up with blisters on her legs and stomach, similar to those of the cold sore virus, and Imogen had eyed them in puzzlement.

'What do you think it is, Doctor?' the patient had asked anxiously.

'I'm not sure,' she'd told her. 'I'm going to ask Dr Nesbitt to have a look at you.'

'I've got a pregnant woman with legs and stomach covered in what looks like the herpes virus,' she'd told him. 'Will you come and have a look?'

He'd just seen a patient and was writing up their notes before calling in the next one. But when he heard what Imogen had to say he put them to one side.

'Of course,' he said with his usual calm confidence, and as she led the way to the nurse's room where the clinic was held asked, 'How's it going?'

Imogen pulled a face. 'We've got it all today. Two with blood pressure that is higher than it should be. A first-timer who's having a bleed at seven months and has been despatched to hospital forthwith. A teenager who can't stop vomiting and now this patient with the strange blisters.'

'It's herpes gestationis,' Blair said when he'd examined her.

'What?' the woman cried hysterically. 'That's a sexually transmitted disease, isn't it? I've never slept with anyone but my husband. If he's been…'

Her voice trailed off and Blair shook his head.

'No. This is nothing like that,' he assured her. 'It might sound similar, but it isn't one of the herpes simplex viruses. It's a rare condition of pregnancy and will disappear once you've had the baby.'

'In the meantime, Dr Rossiter will prescribe a corticosteroid-type drug that should keep it under control as, if left untreated, it can bring on a miscarriage.'

The relief at being told she hadn't picked up something unpleasant was now being wiped out by the mention of the word miscarriage, but again he was there to reassure her.

'Don't worry. We'll monitor the condition carefully and if we think there is the least risk to you or your baby will have you admitted to hospital.'

When she'd left in a chastened state, Imogen said, 'I'd heard of herpes gestationis, but had never come across it until today.'

Blair nodded. 'I've only seen it a few times myself.' He sent a searching glance in her direction. 'Is all this making you nervous about your own pregnancy?'

'No, not at all,' she told him serenely. 'I'm just grateful to be in such good health. And regarding my involvement with the expectant mums, it's better to have one's finger on the pulse than be wandering around in the dark. I'm lucky to be on the inside of things.'

'It's quite clear that you're thinking positively,' he said drily, vaguely irritated that she was coping so well.

She pushed back a lock of dark hair from her brow and observed him with the clear candid gaze that was so much a part of her. He knew why he was feeling rattled. He wanted her to need him. To want him with her, not just now and then but all the time.

That man who'd made her pregnant had no right to have gone off on some fool's errand in the Himalayas, leaving her to face the future alone, he thought morosely, even though he hadn't known about the baby.

If Imogen belonged to him, he would want to be with her all the time. But she didn't belong to him, did she? Didn't want to, or she wouldn't have changed her mind about marrying him.

Maybe if he'd been a bit more passionate about it she would have found the idea more appealing, but it had all happened in a flash. One moment he'd been with her at her father's place merely to give moral support and the next he'd said he was the child's father and had assured Brian Rossiter that there would be a wedding. So who could blame her if he came over as something of a cold customer?

As he brought his mind back to the present she said in a more subdued tone, 'But it doesn't mean that I don't sometimes feel low. Such as when I'm alone in the evenings and I start thinking about what might have been.'

Would Blair pick up on what she meant? she wondered. She was hardly in a position to spell it out. Would he realise that she was telling him how she wished that he was the father of her child and that he'd asked her to marry him for the right reasons?

It was a vain hope.

'I know it's awful for you to have to come to terms with the way your affair with Sean has changed your life,' he said slowly. 'You're brave and, as I've just said, you're thinking positively. You've no idea how I admire you for it.'

She wanted to yell at him, I don't want to be admired. I want to be loved...by you...Blair Nesbitt!

'How about me taking you out somewhere if the evenings are so depressing?' he was saying. 'It would make a change for both of us. Summer is nearly over and before autumn starts to make us feel even more wistful about things that are past, let's escape for a few hours. What do you say?'

Her zest was back.

'I say...yes! Yes!'

'Good. I can't make it tonight as I've promised to do a couple of jobs for Briony, but I'm free tomorrow.'

'Fine,' she agreed immediately, and then took the edge off her pleasure by asking, 'What's she like?'

'Who? Briony?'

'Yes.'

'Tall, slender, long blonde hair, blue eyes and rather introverted.'

'Unlike me, then. I'm an over-confident, undersized, mop-haired, pain in the neck.'

Blair was laughing, mirth rumbling low in his throat.

'Let's just say there are worse things than being a pain in the neck. In the meantime, think about where you'd like me to take you.'

'I'd like to go to the seaside.'

'The coast!' he exclaimed with raised brows. 'It would be dark by the time we got there.'

'Not if we asked Andrew to do the early evening

surgery. We could set off as soon as we've done our home visits.'

'Er…yes…why not?' he agreed, and as one of the receptionists came to inform them that the waiting room was filling up again, he reminded her, 'Don't forget your bucket and spade.'

As he drove home that night Blair was thinking about something that he'd only heard of that day. The medical profession had been researching postnatal depression, the gloom and uncertainty that so often spoilt for the mother those first few weeks of bonding with her child.

Their findings had shown that women with thyroid problems were more likely to be prone to it. It had been suggested that a simple blood test during the gestation period should be done so that the mother-to-be and her medical advisors were aware if she was likely to experience it after the birth.

Fifteen per cent of women who had given birth fell foul of the depressing illness and not all of them recognised what ailed them. They experienced feelings of shame and defeat because they couldn't love their child as they knew they should, blaming it on a lack of affection on their part when in truth it was not their fault at all.

The depression did pass eventually, though in some instances not as quickly as the sufferer would like, and the aftermath of it had often led to the destruction of relationships.

He decided that tomorrow he would discuss it with Imogen. Not because he was expecting her to be affected, although he could hardly blame her if she was, but because it was something they could do for their patients. They could test for thyroid malfunction and if it showed up, the expectant mothers would have a better understanding of a problem that was as old as the hills.

That was one thing he was planning for tomorrow. Another was to spend some time with her away from all their cares and concerns. For a few hours he was going to forget that she was going to bear the child of a dead man and that he was still in a state of limbo as to what he wanted from her.

There was Briony on the sidelines. He always brushed aside any comments regarding her, whether from Simon or Imogen, but he was aware that she was expecting something from him and it wasn't just her odd jobs done.

Maybe he'd overdone the caring friend bit, he thought wryly, but that was what it was going to have to be. She was a nice enough woman but Briony couldn't compete with the bewitching charms of Imogen.

He knew that she was feeling unlovely at the moment and understood why. Yet there was no need for her to feel that way. Like any other pregnant woman, she was allowing her body to be used as a safe harbour for her unborn child until such time as it was ready to set sail on life's sea. And though she might not be aware of it, she was completely desirable as far as he was concerned.

Blair was on his way home to get changed at lunchtime the following day when a call came through on his mobile from the same police station where he had met Imogen on a night in spring.

There had been a death in the cells. He was needed

urgently to verify just how the prisoner had died. Blair sighed. It was going to delay their trip to the coast.

When he tried to ring Imogen there was no answer, which meant that she was still out on her calls. He was glad of it as it meant that she wouldn't be there waiting for him just yet. At that moment he had no idea how long he was going to be at the station.

As soon as he walked into the sombre surroundings of the police station Blair could feel tension and unease in the atmosphere. He knew from past experience that the police didn't like this kind of thing happening on the premises and, whatever he had to say, there would have to be an inquiry.

'I'm the police surgeon,' he told a desk sergeant he'd never met before. 'I believe there's been a death in the cells.'

'Er…yes,' the officer said stiffly, and led the way along a familiar passage. 'Two of the squad brought in a drunk and disorderly earlier this morning and we put him in a cell to sleep it off. When we went to check on him later he was dead.'

'I see.' Blair said grimly, with the clear memory of what had happened to his brother all those years ago. 'They were sure he was drunk, then? It's early in the day for someone to be in that state.'

'Yes, they were sure,' he was told. 'The fellow reeked of it.'

The deceased was lying on the bunk against the back wall of the cell. He was well dressed and groomed and looked to be in his thirties. As they drew near Blair's face tightened. He could see the contorted purple face, the bulging eyes and the dribble of vomit from the man's mouth.

'You didn't need me to tell you what's happened

here,' he said tersely as he felt in vain for a pulse. 'He has choked on his own vomit. How often were your men supposed to check on him?'

The sergeant cleared his throat. 'Every fifteen minutes.'

When Blair eyed him doubtfully he said uncomfortably, 'Except for a short period when we had a rush on. One of the patrols brought in a gang of hooligans who'd been smashing shop windows and it was a bit hectic for a while…and we can't be in two places at once, Doc.'

'Maybe not,' Blair conceded, 'but it is my job to protect the safety and well-being of those locked up. That's what they employ us for and I'm not going to say any different than this fellow choked on his own vomit.'

'We'll have the chief constable going spare when he hears about this,' the other man muttered. 'It reflects on the station.'

'Yes, I'm sure it does,' Blair told him flatly, 'but bear in mind there is a dead man here, Sergeant, who might still be alive if he'd been properly looked after. And now, as there is nothing I can do for the poor fellow, let's get on with the formalities, shall we?'

When Imogen saw his expression she didn't ask Blair why he was late. She'd been watching the afternoon tick away in disappointed exasperation, and when he'd finally pulled up outside the apartments she'd been out there in a flash and strapping herself into the passenger seat before he had a chance to speak.

But the silence had continued to prevail and after covering the first few miles with no words between them she gave up and asked, 'So who's upset you?'

'Your father's lot,' he told her grimly. 'I was called out to a death in the cells. The fellow had choked on his own vomit. What a waste of a life!'

'There are always two sides to everything, Blair,' she said placatingly. 'We're all guilty of human error at one time or another. They don't know from one minute to the next who's going to come rolling into the police station and from being slack one moment, the next every member of the force can be occupied, very often with violent and nasty people.'

'It doesn't alter the fact that our function is to protect those in custody when they can't help themselves,' he said in the same grim tone. 'I know it was too late for me to help that poor guy back there, but it rankles that such a thing could happen in a police station full of personnel.'

'You can rest assured that my father will instigate a full inquiry,' she said, still in placatory mood. 'Whatever else he is, he's an honourable man. And now can we remember that we're supposed to be out to enjoy ourselves?' she asked wistfully, as the delight of having him to herself dwindled with each passing minute.

'Yes, of course,' he said with the restraint still upon him. 'I shouldn't be taking my annoyance out on you. But we are both police surgeons, Imogen. Surely you can see my point.'

'Well, yes, I can,' she agreed, with the feeling that this wasn't going to be a happy outing. 'I suppose it reminded you of what happened to your brother. But this fellow *was* under the influence I presume.'

'Yes, from the smell of him, and anyone who lets themselves get into that state from drinking is a fool…but to end up dead!'

'Shall we turn back?' she asked glumly.

He took his eyes off the road for a second.

'What for?'

'Well, if you're going to be in this mood all the time we're out, we might as well forget it.'

Removing his hand from the steering-wheel, Blair held her clenched fist briefly.

'I'm sorry, Imogen. It's just the way I am,' he said bleakly. 'If the opportunity is there for me to be of service to someone and I'm not given the chance, it really gets to me.'

'Like when you offered to marry me to stave off my father's annoyance?'

He glanced at her sharply. 'I suppose you could say that.'

Suddenly she wanted to strike out at him. She didn't want to be reminded that he'd seen her as a charity case.

'You must have been out of your mind!'

'Yes, I suppose I must have been,' he agreed equably, 'but when I first met you I didn't know that you had a hidden agenda and by the time I found out it was too late.'

'Too late for what?' she breathed, but it seemed that there was still no joy to come.

'Too late not to feel responsible for you.'

'I see.' And turning her head away from him, she spent the rest of the journey with eyes fixed on the passing landscape.

'Do you want to eat first or should we enjoy the last two hours of sunshine before darkness falls?' Blair asked as he parked the car on the seafront.

Imogen was perking up now that they'd finally arrived and when he said, 'I've brought a picnic meal,' her face lit up in surprised pleasure.

'When did you find time to do that?' she exclaimed.

He smiled, his earlier moroseness having diminished.

'I prepared it before I went to the practice this morning and popped it into the fridge.'

Imogen groaned.

'It takes me all my time to have a shower, gulp down a coffee and get there on time. You are just too perfect for words.'

Her voice had softened and she wondered if he realised just how much she meant it. Blair was perfect. Perfect for her. What a pity that she wasn't perfect for him.

Unable to resist asking, she probed, 'Don't you ever do anything crazy or stupid, Blair?'

He smiled. 'I'm here with you, aren't I?'

'And that's crazy...stupid?'

'Maybe.'

'Well, if it isn't already, shall we make it so?' she said laughingly. 'The tide's coming in and the water looks so inviting. I've brought my costume and the label boasts that it's stretch material, so hopefully I'll be able to get into it. What about you?'

'Yes. I've got my swimming shorts.'

'So let's grab a bathing hut and get changed, or we might end up swimming in the dark.'

'Don't look at me,' she entreated as she eased herself out of the loose top and jeans she was wearing.

'Why not?' he breathed softly. 'You're not ashamed of your shape, are you? You shouldn't be. Nearly all the great artists have painted pregnant women. Conception and birth are magical...beyond belief.'

Imogen shrugged smooth shoulders. 'I don't want to start thinking back to this particular conception, and as to the birth, I'll think about that when I have to. I only care about this moment, here with you. If you can stand seeing my nakedness, Blair, come and put your hands on me and feel the child moving inside me.'

He came across and stood before her and she thought that whatever *she* looked like, he was beautiful. Lean and strong-boned, broad-chested and trim-hipped. She ached for her self-imposed celibacy to be over.

His touch was gentle, reverent almost.

'Fantastic!' he breathed as he felt the movement beneath the taut skin. Then his hands moved to her breasts, caressing their ripe fullness and teasing the nipples into rosy hardness. As he kissed each one in turn she whispered, 'You know I want you to make love to me, don't you?'

'Yes,' he said. 'I do. But you know I'm not going to, don't you?'

'Yes. I do.'

'So let's go and frolic in the sea, and once we've had our fill we'll get dried off and have a picnic.'

The sun was ready to set and most of those who'd been there when they'd arrived had wandered off for their evening meal, so they had the beach almost to themselves.

For once Imogen was content. She understood why Blair hadn't made love to her. But maybe one day, she thought dreamily as the waves lapped against her feet, maybe one day he would see her in a different light and then the possibilities would be endless.

They sat on the last strip of dry sand in the warm late summer darkness and ate the meal that he'd brought. Salad, sandwiches, fresh fruit and cream…and champagne.

Imogen wanted it to go on forever, but the moonlit water was edging nearer with every wave that came crashing in and at last Blair said, 'We better pack up or what's left of the picnic will be washed out to sea and us with it.'

She stretched her arms up to the heavens and said softly, 'I know. We started off on a low note but ever since we arrived here it's been magical. I won't forget this day, Blair. It's so long since I enjoyed myself I'd almost forgotten what it feels like.'

He smiled at her in the darkness.

'So we'll have to do it again?'

'Yes, please,' she breathed.

When they got back to her apartment she asked him in but he shook his head and told her, 'I've already resisted temptation once today. I don't want to have to hang onto my resolves again. I'll see you tomorrow. And, Imogen…'

'Yes?' she said expectantly.

'Make sure that the door is securely locked when I've gone.'

'Yes,' she said again, with meek obedience taking the place of anticipation. Even though she wasn't quite sure what it was she'd been anticipating.

The bright bubble of happiness burst two days later. On another warm evening Imogen was shopping in the local supermarket on her way home from the practice when a voice from behind her said, 'I believe you're Imogen Rossiter.'

Swinging round in surprise, she found herself face to face with a tall, solemn-looking blonde.

'You may have heard Blair speak of me. I'm Briony Matthews,' she explained. 'Could I have a word?'

'Yes, of course,' Imogen said breezily from behind her shopping trolley, thinking that she didn't know what impending doom felt like but could make a guess.

'You're pregnant, I believe,' the other woman said coolly.

'Well, I'm certainly not this shape normally,' Imogen said with a smile. 'What can I do for you? Though before you answer, why don't we move across to the café? We are rather causing a blockage with our trolleys.'

'Yes, quite so,' Briony agreed. 'Can I get you a coffee?'

'No, thanks just the same,' Imogen told her. 'It's been a long day at the practice and I'm anxious to get home.'

'Right, I'll get to the point,' she said. 'Blair and I have become very close since my husband died and I would like to know if the child that you're carrying is his.'

As Imogen's face stretched in amazement she went on, 'I wasn't aware that you existed until yesterday, when I went to consult Andrew Travis and was astounded to hear from him that at one time Blair and yourself were contemplating marriage, but have postponed it until after your child is born.'

Imogen goggled at her. She could do without this. The third degree from someone who obviously thought she had a claim on Blair.

Yet maybe she had. He hadn't been very forthcoming when this woman's name had been mentioned previously, so perhaps there was something between them and he wasn't prepared to say.

But where did that leave her, apart from feeling devastated at the thought of him with someone else? Should she tell Briony the truth? That the baby wasn't his, which would make him look somewhat foolish in front of all those who'd been led to believe it was. Or did she go along with the charade they'd got themselves involved in and tell this woman who had appeared out of the blue that he was the father.

'I suspect that this is entrapment,' her blonde inquisitor was saying. 'The result of a one-night stand maybe, and you see the opportunity to ensnare him. Blair is a very special man who doesn't normally sleep around, but I suppose we all make mistakes some time and if a woman told him that her child was his he would do the honourable thing.'

Imogen was in the grip of anger now. How dared this woman say such things about her? Entrapment! She was jumping to conclusions and poking her nose into her affairs at the same time.

Briony needed to be told that any involvement between Blair and herself had been more than willingly agreed to on his part, and if he did have an arrangement with the widow of his friend, so be it. But she was damned if she was going to let herself be judged by a stranger who knew nothing about her.

'As you surmise, my pregnancy is the result of a one-night stand,' she said coolly, 'but it is no business of yours whatsoever. If you are so keen to know my child's parentage, I suggest that you ask Blair himself instead of intruding into my life.'

She got to her feet. 'And now you must excuse me. As I said before, I've had a long and busy day.' And with her head held high and anger still churning inside her, she made her way to the checkout.

*   *   *

The outrage was still there when Imogen got to the practice the next morning, and when Blair saw her set expression he said mildly, 'So who's rubbed you up the wrong way, Dr Rossiter?'

'You do well to ask, Dr Nesbitt,' she told him snappily.

'I presume that I'm supposed to know what you mean by that, but I'm afraid I don't,' he retaliated with a questioning smile.

'Does the name Briony Matthews ring a bell?'

'Yes. Of course it does. You know very well she's a friend of mine. Or at least her husband was. But I'm afraid that you've still got me guessing. What about her?'

'She waylaid me in the supermarket last night and interrogated me about who the father of my child is. You've certainly got a champion there. That woman sees you as the victim of an unscrupulous one-night stand with someone who's out to trawl you into her net. I've never been so insulted in the whole of my life. Especially as the truth of the matter is the exact opposite.

'It's clear that she wants you on any terms. She said that the two of you have an understanding and hinted that she would be willing to forgive you for whatever you've been up to with me. Can you believe it?'

'And what did you tell her?' he asked with deadly calm.

'I told her to ask you if she wanted to know who fathered my child. I didn't know what else to say. I would have preferred to tell her the truth, but thought it might get back to this place and then everyone would know we'd been deliberately misleading them.'

'I see.'

Imogen glared at him.

'Is that all you've got to say? What about an explanation as to why that woman thinks she has a claim on you…and why she thinks she has the right to question me? She hasn't got those ideas from nowhere.'

'So you think she's got them from me?'

'Well! Has she?'

'Look, Imogen,' he said heavily, 'I'm sorry about what happened. Briony has been in a very emotional state ever since she lost her husband and—'

'I don't know about her being emotional,' Imogen butted in angrily. 'Predatory might be a better word to describe her. She accused me of entrapment. Me! The one who let you off the hook with regard to the wedding!'

'Let me off the hook!' he said with the dangerous calm upon him once more. 'I don't know which is worse—being likened to a fish, squirming to get back into the water again, or being fought over like some prize in a raffle. If Briony is predatory, you, Imogen Rossiter, are ungrateful. And now, if it isn't too much trouble, perhaps you'd like to start morning surgery.'

'My pleasure,' she snapped back, 'and tell your lady friend to keep away from me in future…and the same applies to you.'

CHAPTER EIGHT

As SOON as the words were out Imogen wished she could take them back. Briony to stay away from her, yes, but not Blair, never him.

She wanted him more than she'd ever wanted anything, but the moment she began to hope that there was life after pregnancy for them both something always got in the way. This time in the form of another woman who seemed to think that he belonged to her.

One thing she did know about Blair was that there was no deceit in him. If he was involved with Briony and hadn't felt the necessity to tell her about it, it would be because she wasn't all that important to him. And if that was the case, what was she going to do about it? Nothing?

He was turning away and she reached out to him, but he shrugged off her detaining hand and, closing the door of his consulting room behind him with a decisive click, left her to her regrets.

When surgery was over she tried to waylay him in the passage outside their rooms but he was reluctant to talk. With a smile that had a trace of weariness in it he said, 'Leave it, Imogen. I think you've said all that needs to be said.'

'That's just it!' she protested. 'I haven't. I didn't…'

His jawline tightened.

'I said forget it. I've a list of calls as long as my arm and so have you.'

'So you're not going to tell me what's going on between Briony and yourself.'

'Would you believe me if I did?'

'Try me.'

'Listen, you aggravating woman,' he growled. 'We have work to do. Stop pestering me about things that you know nothing about.'

'That's exactly it! I don't know and I should.'

'By whose authority?'

'Mine! Because I'm in love with you…head over heels. And don't tell me that because I'm carrying another man's child I'm not entitled to feel like that.'

His face had whitened and Imogen thought dismally that he wasn't exactly bubbling over with joy at the news, but he wouldn't be, would he? Not if he had something going with Briony…and not when he considered what marrying *her* would entail. He might have been thinking along those lines once, but it hadn't been mentioned since.

'Would you have time to see Mrs Cathcart before you go on your rounds, Dr Rossiter?' one of the receptionists was asking. 'She's asked to see a woman doctor.'

'Has she got an appointment?' Imogen asked edgily. Morning surgery was supposed to be over and she was desperate to talk to Blair. The receptionist shook her head.

'No. She's just arrived and seems very agitated.'

'Of course Dr Rossiter will see her,' Blair said smoothly, as if unaware how desperate she was to talk and picking up his bag he went.

'So what's the problem?' she asked a few minutes later, smiling reassuringly, as a chalky-faced, thirty-plus housewife seated herself opposite.

The moment Jackie Cathcart had presented herself Imogen had felt guilty about her reluctance to see her but now she was ready to put her own problems to one side and listen to someone else's.

'I'm pregnant, Doctor.'

'And is that a problem?' Imogen asked carefully, taking note of the way the patient was twisting a small cotton handkerchief between her fingers.

'Yes. It is. My husband has multiple sclerosis and is confined to a wheelchair. The baby isn't his. I've been having an affair.'

'I see,' Imogen said slowly.

'I doubt it,' she said tearfully. 'I was lonely and feeling unloved and was stupid enough to think that a man who was fit and strong could make up for what my husband can't give me.'

'Does your husband know?'

She shuddered.

'No. He's bitter enough already. It would finish him off completely.'

'So what is it that you want, Mrs Cathcart?' Imogen asked, as if she didn't know.

'I want an abortion.'

'Have you any other children?'

'No. Nigel became ill shortly after we were married and babies just weren't on the agenda then. Now we couldn't have one if we wanted to.'

'And your husband wouldn't want to bring up another man's child?' she asked with the feeling that this scenario had familiar overtones.

'That's just it. He couldn't even if he wanted to. He's too ill.'

'We don't advise anyone to rush into a termination,' she told her gently. 'How far along are you?'

'I've missed two periods.'

'I'd like to examine you. Sometimes when a woman is under great stress she doesn't menstruate for that reason.'

Jackie eyed her bleakly.

'I've done the home pregnancy test and it was positive.'

'Let's just be sure, though, shall we?'

When she'd done the internal examination Imogen nodded. 'I wish I could have told you otherwise, but I'm afraid that you are pregnant.'

'So let's get the abortion sorted,' Jackie pleaded.

'Time *is* getting short,' Imogen agreed, 'but you must give yourself a few more days to think it over. I could arrange for counselling if you wish. You know there are other choices you could consider, such as adoption.'

'It's all right for the likes of you,' the other woman said wearily. 'You've got someone to support you in your pregnancy. I believe that you and Dr Nesbitt are a couple.'

I wish! Imogen thought, and hedged. 'Er…yes…we are to a degree, but that doesn't mean that we will stay that way. But getting back to your problem, Jackie, let me know what you decide and if you still want to go ahead I'll recommend you for the termination.'

'All right,' the woman agreed reluctantly, 'but I can't see how I can change my mind. I just can't bring any more misery into Nigel's life.'

'And what about the baby's father?' Imogen asked. 'What does he have to say.'

'He's long gone. It was a stupid mad fling that only lasted a matter of days and I should have known better.'

That makes two of us, Imogen thought. Since she'd met Blair, she'd discovered what a real man was like, and he certainly put the rest of them in the shade as far as she was concerned.

She was a fool to have let her annoyance with his predatory blonde friend cause a rift between them. But there were worse things to worry about than that. Supposing that he did care for the woman. Life with Briony would be more tranquil than taking someone like herself for his soul mate.

As Blair did his rounds he was ruminating on what had gone on with Imogen back at the practice. He understood her annoyance at being cross-examined by Briony, but instead of offering reassurance he'd been tense and angry...but not with her. Not with the captivating witch who had him constantly bemused.

He should have made it clear to Briony long ago how they stood. But she had clung to him in her grief and he'd held back from explaining that he was merely there to help her through a bad patch. Now it was too late. She'd made her move.

He'd been expecting it, but not with Imogen as piggy in the middle. He felt that Briony had a cheek, accosting Imogen in the supermarket of all places, but it was done and the first chance he got she was going to be told that she'd presumed too much.

His mouth twisted at the memory of Imogen's outburst. She'd said she loved him...or thought she did more likely. She was in a very vulnerable state at the moment and her meeting with Briony hadn't helped. But it wasn't the time for protestations of love.

Her thoughts should be on other things at this time. Facing up to giving birth without the child's father present. Getting ready to adjust to the new routines of motherhood so that she could hold onto the job and care for her child at the same time.

Blair hoped that her father was going to shape up soon. She needed all the help she could get and that old tartar was backward at coming forward to say the least.

Bringing the chief constable to mind brought forth recollections of the dead man in the cells. He'd heard no further on that matter, but felt that he might be asked to appear at any inquiry that was set up by the police authority.

Yet there would be little he could tell them. It was always on the cards that someone hopelessly drunk might choke on vomit and it had been a clear-cut instance of that very thing.

Other memories of that particular day were far more pleasant. Imogen in rounded nakedness begging him not to look, when he could no more have turned away than flown to the moon.

She'd invited him to feel the child moving inside her and he'd ached for it to be his. He asked himself sometimes why he was such a glutton for punishment. Why couldn't he have been attracted to a woman less provoking, less complicated…less pregnant? In other words…Briony Matthews.

When Blair got back Imogen was missing and Lauren said, 'Dr Rossiter was called out on police business. She doesn't expect to be away long.'

He sighed. At bordering on eight months pregnant Imogen could have passed it on to him, but remembering her mood of earlier he supposed that was the last thing she would have considered doing.

'What was it? Do you know?'

Lauren nodded.

'A man was taken ill as he was being transported to the police station. He was so violent when a young WPC tried to arrest him that she used CS gas to restrain him and he was badly affected.'

She was observing his grim expression.

'I suggested to Imogen that she pass it on to you, but she said that she was concerned in case the suspect took a turn for the worse and there was a delay in one of you getting there.'

'They should have taken him right to hospital,' he said tightly, and knew he was letting his anxiety over Imogen get the better of him. But was it ever going to be any different?

Once she'd given birth she would be free to go where she wanted. To be with who she wanted. To work where she wanted. And where would that leave him? Certainly not in the role of prospective bridegroom.

She'd changed her mind about marrying him faster than the speed of light, so obviously she had no hankerings in that direction. Yet today she'd said she loved him. What was she trying to do? Rattle him? Get him to make a move? And then what—turn him down again?

At that moment Imogen came breezing in and he said tightly, 'I could have done that.'

'Yes, I know you could,' she agreed levelly with the frost of their earlier disagreement still upon her, 'but I was the one they sent for—needlessly as it turned out. The fellow was all right when I got there.

'I called in at my father's office while I was on that side of the city. Celia phoned last night to say that he hasn't been well and would I drop in on him on the pretext that I was passing by.'

'And?'

'He said he was all right. Wouldn't let me examine him, but he's promised to come to see you later this afternoon. Typically, he wouldn't want to be treated by an underling, even if it was his own daughter.'

Blair's smile was tinged with irony. 'I'll tell Reception to get out the red carpet, then.'

He'd only seen the chief constable once since allowing him to think he was the father of Imogen's child and wasn't looking forward to meeting him again, but he was a patient and, as such, must be treated.

High colour, breathlessness, lack of energy. Part of the aging heart syndrome, Blair thought as he told the older man he could put his shirt back on.

'You're going to have to take some time off,' he told Imogen's father. 'I presume you have private health care?' The other man nodded. 'Right. I'm sending you to see a cardiologist.'

'Fair enough,' Brian agreed. 'But I don't intend taking time off. I need to have my finger on the pulse where the police force is concerned.'

'I've just had my finger on your pulse,' Blair told him levelly, 'and as with your breathlessness and general weakness, it tells me that here is a man who has to slow down. You do want to live to see this grandchild of yours, don't you?'

'Yes, of course I do,' Brian said irritably.

'So let's make sure that you do. I picked up a heart murmur when I listened to your chest. It could be caused by various things but I suspect a valve problem, which is often due to a narrowing of the arteries that comes with age. The consultant will request that your chest be X-rayed and that an ECG be done. He will almost certainly also ask for echocardiography to be performed.'

'And what might that be?'

'It is a harmless and pain-free process. A transducer, an instrument that picks up and sends out signals, is placed upon the chest in such a way that it allows sound waves to reach the part of the heart under investigation. The echoes it picks up are then amplified and displayed on a screen for the cardiologist to make his interpretation of how the heart valves are working. The most common problems found in that area are aortic or pulmonary stenosis.'

'So if I do have a valve problem, what's the score?' the chief constable asked.

'It would depend on the seriousness of the defect. Sometimes surgery is used to widen the narrowed area. In more urgent situations a new metal valve is inserted to replace the faulty one.'

'I see. So with a bit of luck I might be around for a while longer.'

Blair smiled.

'I'm sure you will. Your wife needs you and so does Imogen…and then there's the first of the new generation of Rossiters that will shortly be arriving.'

'Aye. I wish it was under different circumstances, though.'

Don't we all? Blair thought ruefully, but he wasn't going to explain to Imogen's father what his feelings were on the matter.

'Is Imogen around?' the other man asked as he got to his feet.

'She's taking the antenatal clinic. I can take over for her if you want to have a word.'

Brian shook his head.

'No, don't disturb her. You must both come to dine with us soon. She won't have much time once the er…er…child…is born.'

'Imogen needs you. You do know that, don't you?' Blair told him. 'She's very vulnerable at the moment, which is not surprising, and needs all the support she can get. These are times when families have to stick together.'

'Are you lecturing me, Nesbitt?' the other man asked curtly as the mantle of police chief settled back onto his shoulders. 'Because, if you are, there's no need. I know my responsibilities.

'But I have to say, why the devil did you let Imogen call off the wedding? You must have some feelings for her or you wouldn't have asked her to marry you. I would have been delighted to have you for a son-in-law.'

He was ready to shake hands and depart but had one last thing to say.

'I want to see this cardiac fellow today if possible. Tomorrow at the latest.'

'I'll see what I can do,' Blair promised with the unexpected vote of confidence still ringing in his ears. 'I'll phone your home as soon as I've sorted something out.'

'So, what was wrong with the mighty one?' Imogen asked when the clinic was over.

'I detected a heart murmur. Possibly a valve not functioning as it should,' Blair told her. 'I've promised to make an immediate appointment for him to see a cardiólogist.'

She sighed. 'Dad won't like having anything wrong with him. He thinks he's invincible. Do you know, he would rather read the crime statistics than a good book? I can't possibly visualise what he'll be like with the baby. He'll probably want me to teach the child the Highway Code before introducing it to nursery rhymes.'

She was laughing but Blair felt it was strained. Imogen was concerned about her father and that was how it should be. He only hoped that Rossiter would feel the same when the time came for her to give birth.

As if reading his thoughts, she was eyeing him defiantly, challenging him to say them out loud, but as he had no intention of doing so it was left to her to break the silence.

But when he looked up the defiance had gone and tears were streaming down her cheeks.

'Everything is such a mess,' she sobbed. 'Me in this situation. My dad, who has never had a thing wrong with him in his life, maybe needing heart surgery, and you in the clutches of that nosy blonde!'

If she hadn't been so upset he would have wanted to laugh.

'Come here,' he said gently. 'Let me wipe away the tears. And while I'm doing so let me put you straight about my strength of character. I am not in anybody's ''clutches''. The other day you referred to letting me off the hook and now I'm in Briony's clutches. What sort of a jellyfish do you think I am, my raven-haired witch? You need to have patience where you and I are concerned and spend less time jumping to conclusions.

'As to the ''mess'' you're in with regard to the baby,

it's only a "mess" if you let it become one. And your father isn't at death's door exactly. I shall keep a close watch on him. I've had patients with his problem before. So have you and they've usually made a good recovery once the valve has been sorted out. I saw a patient the other day who's had a metal heart valve for over thirty years and apart from it doing a bit of rocking and rolling sometimes its still going strong, so you see…'

'I know,' she sniffled contritely. 'You are always the voice of reason while I seem to be waffling along in a muddle that's all blacks and greys.'

'Nonsense!' he said briskly. 'You're bright and beautiful…brave and funny…'

'Don't!' she cried. 'You know you don't really think that. But thanks just the same…Dr Nesbitt.' And with the smile that had ensnared him from the first moment of meeting she pressed her lips to his cheek.

He could smell her perfume. The touch of her mouth against his stubble was as light as thistledown and twice as disturbing. He turned his head, saw the message in her eyes, and incredibly laughter was replacing tears.

As he observed her questioningly she gurgled, 'If you're going to kiss me, you'll either have to lean over the bump or do it from the side.'

He found himself joining in her laughter, and as passion was overruled by mirth they let the light-hearted moment take over until Andrew came in to see what all the noise was about.

When Blair had gone back to his own sanctum and the elderly third member of the practice had left early to get in a round of golf, Imogen prepared to face the late afternoon surgery with a lighter heart than before.

Blair had been right in everything he'd said. Where was her usual drive and optimism these days? she wondered. Did all pregnant women feel in the doldrums during the last few weeks, or was she different because of her situation?

You ought to be grateful that you've got family and a rock like Blair to hold onto, she told herself. What about the teenagers who are pregnant with no one to turn to? Whose boyfriends and families don't want to know and the kids are left to fend for themselves?

She'd had them sitting across the desk from her. Seen them come and go and done what she could for them, while fretting because she couldn't do more.

The following day Imogen was due to go to the city's main hospital for an examination by the obstetrician. She'd seen him twice before without any problems presenting themselves and was expecting today to be the same.

It was.

'The baby's heartbeat is strong. Its position perfect for a natural birth and your blood pressure is fine,' the elderly consultant told her when the examination was over. 'Do you have any questions or problems that you'd like to discuss with me?'

She was feeling more buoyant today and told him with a smile, 'None that you could help me with. Such as persuading the man I'm in love with to love me, too. Or telling my father, the chief constable, to slow down.'

He smiled back.

'Sorry. Not on my agenda. Your man friend must be crazy...and I've heard that Brian Rossiter is a workaholic.'

Outside the hospital a few minutes later she stood on the pavement considering whether to go back to the apartment to eat or have something while she was in the city centre.

The traffic was noisy and everywhere was crowded. A quiet lunch at home was a more appealing prospect than pushing her way through the crowds, she decided.

Two young mothers were standing a few feet away, gossiping animatedly. They both had babies in prams. One of them also had a toddler around her feet, grizzling to be on the move.

Suddenly the child broke free and came racing along the pavement towards Imogen, with the mother in pursuit. As he drew alongside Imogen put out her hand to stop him but he veered sideways and straight into the road.

In that second all she could think of was that she was the nearest. The noise of the traffic was suddenly filled with menace and as a bus loomed up from nowhere with a taxi alongside it she threw herself after the child and, grabbing his arm, flung him back onto the pavement.

There wasn't time to leap to safety herself. In her ungainly state she overbalanced and in the terrifying moment of impact she prayed that in the saving of someone else's child she wasn't going to lose her own.

The late surgery was due to start and Imogen wasn't back. Blair was beginning to feel vaguely uneasy. Had there been some problem at the hospital? he'd wondered. But when he phoned the clinic that she'd attended he was told that she'd been fine and had left some time ago.

Maybe she'd been having another attack of the doldrums and had gone back to the apartment to have a bite and unwind. That was his next surmise after letting another hour go by, but there was no answering voice when he rang.

It was an incoming call that had the answer. He picked up the phone to find her father at the other end of the line, and when he heard the chief constable's voice Blair thought, What does he want now? He'd already been on to him earlier with details of the cardiac appointment and now here he was again.

But what Brian had to say wiped every other thought from his mind.

'Imogen's been hurt…seriously!' he said without preamble. 'She's in A and E. We're here with her, Celia and I. They're trying to save the child but not giving us much hope for either of them.'

Blair looked down at his knuckles. His hand looked like a bleached white claw, so tightly was he gripping the phone.

'I'm on my way,' he said as his blood ran cold with dread.

How? Blair was asking himself frantically as he drove to the hospital. How had Imogen got hurt? He should have asked her father, but there'd been something in Rossiter's voice that had made him feel there was no time to waste.

Had she been attacked? Had a fall? Crashed her car? He would know soon enough. The way of it wasn't all that important. It was how badly hurt she was that mattered. The hospital staff were trying to save them, Brian had said, but weren't offering much hope.

He stopped the car outside the hospital with a screech of brakes and ran like the wind through the grounds to where the sign ACCIDENT AND EMERGENCY stood out in bold blue letters.

The chief constable and his wife were in the waiting room, sitting silently staring into space, and Blair caught his breath. Was he too late? He prayed not.

Celia saw him and touched her husband's arm. When he turned round Blair hardly recognised him, even though he'd seen him only the previous day. He looked old and defeated and Blair thought illogically that if Imogen could see her father now she would know for all time how much he cared.

'How is she?' Blair asked raggedly.

'Holding on,' Celia told him with an anxious glance at her husband. 'But they couldn't save the baby, Blair. They delivered it by Caesarean but it was already dead.'

He sank down onto the nearest chair.

'What happened, for heaven's sake?'

'Imogen went into the road after a toddler that had escaped from his mother and dashed into the traffic stream outside the hospital. She managed to hurl the child to safety, but wasn't quick enough to save herself. A taxi hit her full on.'

'What's the damage?' he asked tersely.

'Fractures, stomach and head injuries. The only good thing about the whole sorry business is that it happened outside this place and she was being treated within minutes.'

'Does Imogen know that she's lost the baby?'

Her father spoke for the first time.

'No. She's still in Theatre.'

'I have to see her,' Blair said desperately.

'She's going to be in there for hours,' Brian said. 'They wouldn't let us anywhere near.'

'I'll see what I can find out,' Blair promised, and went striding off down the corridor in the direction of the operating theatre.

Imogen was out of Theatre and had been transferred to Intensive Care. She hadn't regained consciousness since the accident so mercifully was unaware of the birth—and death—of her baby or the surgery that had been performed in an effort to save her life.

'We've done a good job on the fractures,' the surgeon who'd operated had told them a few moments ago, 'but the head injury is a different matter. She has a fracture of the skull, which as you are probably aware can cause bone fragments to be pushed inwards. So far there are no haematomas present, which is reassuring, but we won't know the full extent of the damage until she comes round.

'It was touch and go for a while when Dr Rossiter was first brought in. She suffered cardiac arrest, but we managed to shock her back to life and then got on with the job of putting her back together.'

I don't believe I'm hearing this, Blair thought as he looked at Imogen's swollen face. They could have lost her. They still might. And Imogen had lost her baby. How was she going to cope with that if she didn't follow it into eternity?

'What was the child?' he asked the surgeon.

'A girl…with lots of dark hair like her mother. She didn't stand a chance. Dr Rossiter was hit head on.'

Brian groaned. Turning to Blair, Celia said anxiously, 'I feel I should take my husband home. He's on the verge of collapse. Can we leave you here to watch over Imogen? We can soon be back if there is any change.'

He nodded.

'Yes, of course. I'm not intending to leave her side. I'll phone the practice and tell them what's happened. Andrew Travis, my partner, will have to hold the fort for the time being.'

When they'd gone he looked down at Imogen's still form. Her head was bandaged. One of her arms was in plaster and both her legs. There'd been a fracture of the pelvis, too, but that wasn't immediately visible.

Her injuries were numerous and a cause for great concern, but he knew if she ever regained consciousness they would pale into insignificance when she realised that her womb was empty.

Andrew rang late in the evening to express his concern and to suggest that they advertise for a locum with all speed.

'Yes, do that,' Brian agreed abruptly.

It was as if the practice was a million miles away. The only realities were Imogen lying motionless beside him, the swift-footed intensive care staff flitting in and out and the trappings of lifesaving equipment all around them.

Was this how it was going to end? he thought wretchedly. His dark enchantress snatched away from him before he'd told her what was in his heart. He was a fool to have wasted all the precious weeks and months since they'd met that night in the police station.

But from the moment that she'd told him she was pregnant he'd been haunted by the thought of her carrying another man's child. He could have loved it, accepted it as his own, but there had always been the concern in him that when she saw him with the baby she would remember that it wasn't his.

So he had steeled himself to wait...to be patient…until such time as she was ready to venture into the uncharted sea of marriage to a man who wasn't her child's father.

And where had it got him? Nowhere, if he lost her.

CHAPTER NINE

IT WAS two o'clock in the morning when Imogen opened her eyes. Hunched by the bed for what had seemed like an eternity of fraught vigilance, Blair felt the balm of sweet relief wash over him.

For the first few seconds she gazed around her blankly. There was no recognition in the beautiful hazel eyes that he'd seen sparkle with both laughter and tears. They were blank and red-rimmed in the pallor of her face.

He said her name softly and without moving her head she transferred her glance to him. He watched as she fought her way through the numb haze that she'd awakened to, and as bleak reality surfaced he reached out to take her uninjured hand in his.

She pushed it weakly away and felt the flat plateau that was now her stomach. Her face twisted.

'Where's my baby, Blair?' she asked through dry lips.

'They couldn't save her,' he said gently. 'They did their best but she was already dead when they delivered her.'

'So it was a girl.'

'Yes.'

'I want to see her.'

'Yes, I know, but first I'm going to ring for the nurse. You're in Intensive Care. They've been in and out for hours checking on you and will want to assess you now that you're back with us.'

He had expected tears but there weren't any. She was dry-eyed as she croaked. 'I killed her! It's my fault! I don't care if I live or die. I shouldn't have done what I did.'

'You only did what anyone else would have done,' he told her firmly. 'And you're going to live, for all our sakes—yours, mine, your father's and Celia's. She's taken him home because he was in such a state.'

Imogen wasn't listening. Her thoughts were in some far-away place that only she could see. She was shutting him out, he thought painfully. Withdrawing into a world that had no place for him.

As the nurses came hurrying in he stepped back into the shadows with the feeling that was where he'd been relegated to. Yet why? She was going to need him in the days ahead. It would be weeks before she was well enough to go home with all the injuries she'd sustained and with a Caesarean section on top of them.

'The consultant will be back to see Dr Rossiter shortly,' the sister in charge told him. 'In the meantime, she needs rest.'

Blair gave a wry smile.

'In other words, you'd like me to go.'

'Just for a little while.'

'Imogen wants to see the baby,' he told her, 'and I think it's important that she does. To say goodbye for one thing, and to help her adjust to the extremely sudden loss of it. What do you advise in her present state?'

'That she is allowed to see it as soon as possible, but not yet. She's not up to it. When we delivered the little one there were no obvious injuries. It was just as if she was sleeping, so there would be no distress for her regarding that, but for any mother in this situation it is a heart-rending moment.

'When we think she can cope with seeing the baby we will bring her to her, and later we can discuss funeral arrangements if she so wishes.'

They'd been having the discussion in low voices away from the bed, but now Blair returned to Imogen's side and, taking her limp hand in his, told her, 'The consultant is coming shortly and they've asked me to leave for a little while. Needless to say, it won't be for long. I'm anxious to hear what he has to say. I promised to ring your father and Celia the moment there was any news so I'll do that on my way home. And, Imogen…'

He paused. She was gazing up at the ceiling and he wondered if she'd heard a word he'd said. But what he had to say next brought her eyes back to him, as he'd thought it might.

'They're going to bring the baby to you soon. Have you chosen a name for her?'

'Mmm. Joy.'

He looked down at the polished floor of the ward and almost groaned out loud. Joy! Had there ever been a more joyless event than this?

'Lovely,' he told her gently, but when he raised his head it was to find that she'd closed her eyes and he was shut out once more.

'Don't worry,' a hovering nurse told him. 'Dr Rossiter's still in deep shock. She will be more like herself as the healing process progresses.'

He sighed.

The nurse was talking about the body. His concerns were about the mind.

When she'd opened her eyes at the bottom of the black pit that she'd kept trying to claw her way out of,

Imogen had known that something dreadful had happened.

It had felt right that Blair's had been the first face she'd seen on awakening. She couldn't have borne it if it had been anyone else's. But the moment she'd touched the flatness where the baby had been she'd wanted to crawl back into the darkness and never come out again.

As the memory of the accident had come flooding back there'd been guilt mingling with her raw grief, the sickening knowledge that once again she'd done something incredibly stupid.

It hadn't been the fates punishing her for all the times she'd wished the pregnancy had never happened. She'd meted out her own punishment and now she was wishing that she'd followed her child into the next world.

All right, she'd saved the toddler, but at what cost. The little boy's mother had only been feet away. She should have let her rescue her own child. Her own response had been a reflex action, which was typical of the way she was. Acting without thinking and then having to live with regret.

Maybe one day she would be able to tell Blair how she was hurting, but not now. In these first few hours of despair she was having to accept that her life would never be the same again. Her light had been extinguished. Her bouncy zest gone. Long empty days lay ahead.

You're worrying too soon, Blair told himself as he drove home for a quick bite and a change of clothes. How did you expect Imogen to behave when she heard that she'd lost her child?

He already knew the answer to that. He'd expected her to need him more than ever. To cling to him in her despair like the lifeline that he wanted to be for her. But he was being ridiculous.

As someone who came into contact with the quirks and foibles of the human mind all the time in the course of his work, he should know better than anyone that shock and injury often brought about strange behaviour.

Simon was on the point of letting himself in when Blair got home, and his younger brother observed him in surprise.

'And where have you been until this late hour?' he asked. 'Not at the police station again?'

Blair shook his head. 'No. I've just come from the hospital. Imogen has lost the baby.'

'So it was yours.'

'In everything but blood...yes,' he informed him abruptly.

Simon was eyeing him questioningly. 'You're in love with her, aren't you? Have been all along.'

'Yes, if you really want to know.'

'We could have a double wedding,' his brother suggested tactlessly.

Blair glared at him. 'What do you mean by that?'

'Lauren and I got engaged tonight.'

'That's great news,' he said, dredging up a smile, 'but you're going to need a sensitivity transplant if it's going to work.'

'Huh? What do you mean?'

'That you should be talking about my marrying Imogen at a moment like this. She's devastated by what has happened.'

Simon had the grace to look ashamed.

'Sorry,' he mumbled. 'It just seemed...'

'Give it a rest, will you?' Blair snapped back, and flung himself under the shower.

They'd taken Imogen's handbag into the hospital with her at the time of the accident and Blair had told Celia on the phone that he would take her door key and call at the apartment to pick up some clothes and toiletries for her.

He'd also impressed upon the nursing staff that he wanted to be there when she saw the baby. Whether she wanted him around or not, he knew he had to be there. His heart ached for her. There seemed to be so little he could do.

When he arrived at the apartment he quickly gathered what was needed and was about to leave when the smell of paint caught his nostrils. He paused. The door of the spare room was ajar and when he pushed it open he saw that it was half-decorated in nursery paper.

There were paint pots on the window-sill and a trestle table with a bucket of paste resting at one end. Draped over the stepladder was a paint-splashed smock. Reaching across for it, he pressed it against his cheek and wept for the waste of it all.

When he got back to the hospital Celia and Brian were there. Blair was relieved to see that Imogen's father had perked up, although he was still a long way from looking his usual brisk self.

'They let us see Imogen for a few moments,' Celia said, 'and she's asked us to arrange Joy's funeral for when the consultant decides she's well enough to attend.'

She glanced at her husband who was gazing sombrely through a window in the hospital corridor. 'Brian is relieved that there is at least something he can do for her and the baby. It was a terrible moment when they brought it to her.'

'She's seen her!' he exclaimed with the feeling that he'd just been struck a blow to the heart.

'Yes,' Celia said tearfully. 'Just for a few moments. She was too weak to hold her any longer.'

'I see,' he said slowly. And he did. He saw quite clearly that the moment he'd gone Imogen had asked to see the baby again and the nurses had ignored his request.

He knew he couldn't blame them. He had no claim on her. They would know by now that he wasn't Joy's father. That he wasn't married or engaged to Imogen. In fact, he was a nobody in the present situation.

But there was no sign of his ravaged emotions as he approached her bed once more. All that mattered was Imogen…that her distress be curtailed as much as possible and that her body should heal. He would cope with the aftermath of what had happened when those two things had been accomplished.

'Just a few moments with the patient if you don't mind, Dr Nesbitt,' the sister said when he'd arrived at the ward. 'The consultant has seen Imogen and so far is pleased with her progress. There doesn't seem to be any brain damage from the fractured skull, which is most fortunate, and as for the stomach injuries and broken bones, we shall be keeping a close watch on them. But as we both knew, it's early days yet.'

'Yes. I keep telling myself that,' he told her sombrely.

As Blair began to move towards the bed she called

him back and said in a low voice, 'I'd like a quick word before you leave.'

'So you've seen Joy,' he said gently after he'd planted a kiss on what could be seen of Imogen's brow.

Again there were no tears. She just nodded and turned her head away.

'Was she beautiful?'

Another nod was all he got, and now she'd closed her eyes.

'I've just seen your father and Celia,' he told her without referring to the baby again.

He felt like an inarticulate acquaintance instead of someone who adored the ground she walked on, and knew he wasn't coping as well as he should.

He didn't stay long. He knew the staff wanted Imogen kept quiet during these first hours of recovery and also he still sensed that she didn't want him there.

But it wasn't going to keep him away. He would go insane if she started asking that he should not be allowed to visit.

'What was it you had to say to me?' he asked the sister on his way out.

'I just wanted to explain that we didn't ignore your request that you be there when Imogen saw her baby,' she said apologetically. 'It was at her insistence that you weren't present.'

He managed the grimace of a smile.

'No problem. I understand. The last thing I want to do is upset her.'

It was Saturday and, though he had little inclination to do so, Blair called in at the practice to see what was happening there.

The short weekend surgery had just finished and

Andrew met him with a worried, slightly petulant expression on his face, which Blair concluded had something to do with missing some time on the golf course.

'I've been in touch with George Redvers, a retired colleague of mine, who will come in to cover Dr Rossiter's absence if that is all right with you,' he said.

'I'd want to speak to him first,' Blair told him.

Whatever was going on in his private life, the integrity of the practice was very important to him and taking on new staff at a moment's notice was something he rarely did.

'George is picking me up in a few moments,' Andrew said. 'We're off to the golf club. How about having a chat with him while he's here?'

Blair frowned. He was in no mood for it, but he supposed it was a good idea to meet the prospective locum while he had the chance.

When George had gone Blair breathed a sigh of relief. That was one thing sorted. If only the rest of the things that plagued his mind could be dealt with so easily.

After Blair had gone, Imogen slowly opened her eyes and found herself looking up into the face of a perplexed nurse.

'What's with you and Dr Nesbitt?' she asked. 'He's worried sick about you and you don't seem to care.'

Care! Imogen thought wretchedly. It was caring that was weighing her down like a leaden rock. The aching love for her baby, who'd had to be hastened into the world before its time and then not lived to see it.

And there was her love for Blair, a separate, precious thing that for some reason she didn't want to think about during these dark days.

She knew he'd told the staff that he wanted to be there for her when she was shown the baby, but she knew that she didn't want that. He'd distanced himself ever since finding out she was pregnant and she couldn't blame him.

She'd had to put her hopes and dreams of being with him on hold because she'd been pregnant…and so had he. But none of it had been the fault of the defenceless baby that she'd lost. *She* knew that, but did he?

If only she could run away and hide, she kept thinking, away from all the pain and uncertainty. But in plaster casts and bandages there wasn't much chance of that.

The odd thing was that her father's presence was more acceptable than Blair's these days. Probably because for once he was demanding nothing of her.

Amazingly he'd had nothing to say but words of encouragement, urging her to get better soon, and she hadn't the heart to tell him that she wasn't bothered whether she did or not.

The family of the child she'd saved had been to see her. Seeing their distress at the consequences of her brave action, she'd felt bound to try to lighten their guilt.

'I did what anyone would have done,' she'd told them weakly. 'You have nothing to blame yourselves for.'

As the days passed, Blair visited Imogen once daily in the evenings, which left him time to keep the practice on an even keel.

George Redvers was an asset in her absence. He was pleasant and capable and the patients liked him, which helped to ease Blair's burden.

He would have visited her more often but it was still there, the feeling that she didn't want to see him. So he left the daytimes free for her father and Celia and spent a short time with her each evening.

She still had the plaster casts on her arm and legs, but her other injuries were healing and her strength was slowly returning with each passing day.

Their conversations were pleasant enough. They chatted about everything under the sun except themselves, and Blair accepted that it was how she wanted it.

A lot of the time they talked about the practice. He sensed that Imogen felt safe when work was the topic, though she never mentioned coming back and he was now looking at her return from the point of view of 'if' rather than 'when'.

He had steeled himself to wait, convinced that one day the woman he'd fallen in love with would be waiting when he walked into the ward, but so far she was still absent.

'Did Jackie Cathcart ever come back to arrange a termination?' she asked one night.

He shook his head.

'Not to my knowledge. I could check her notes to see if she's seen either Andrew or George, but somehow I don't think so. Why do you ask?' he wanted to know.

'She's got a very sick husband and had had an affair, ending up pregnant. She was adamant that she wanted a termination, but I asked her to consider it for a little while and I've been hoping that she decided against it.'

He'd been watching her carefully to see if the discussion was upsetting her, but she was perfectly calm and for the thousandth time he wondered what was going on in her mind.

The following night she told him with the same lack of emotion that the consultant had said she was well enough to attend Joy's funeral and that it had been arranged for the next day.

'It's in the morning, so I'll understand if you can't be there because of the practice,' she told him, and for the first time since the accident he let his frustration show.

'Of course I'll be there,' he said stiffly. 'Joy wasn't my child, but I've been involved enough in your pregnancy to feel I have some entitlement to be there and I will be. Even though I know you'd rather I didn't attend.'

She swallowed hard and, ashamed of his irritation, he thought how frail she was.

'I know I'm being difficult,' she said, 'but I can't help it, Blair. I have this feeling that I'm being punished for falling in love with you.'

'Why, for heaven's sake?' he exclaimed. 'If you are being punished then so am I. Why does life with you have to be so complicated, Imogen?'

'I don't know,' she said bleakly, and his anger melted like snow in the sun.

In an attempt to bring a lighter note into the conversation he reminded her that she had been invited to Simon's forthcoming wedding to Lauren, which was to take place in the late autumn.

It had been a vain hope. She just shrugged and said, 'I might go if I'm out of here in time. At least it isn't a christening.'

As he drove home that night his spirits were at their lowest ebb. He couldn't believe that Imogen didn't want him at Joy's funeral. It was the final snub. The straw that broke the camel's back.

Yet he couldn't give up on her. He would grit his teeth and carry on hoping. There was nothing else he could do. What Imogen was suffering from was a more complex thing than postnatal depression. It was grief that wasn't being allowed to run its course because of needless guilt.

Brian, who Blair felt had mellowed somewhat in recent days, rang to discuss the funeral shortly after he arrived home.

'I shall be there,' Blair told the older man. 'Though I'm not sure how welcome I will be. In Imogen's eyes I'm connected with what happened to Joy. It breaks my heart to see her distress, but she won't let me get near her. I'm hoping that after the little one has been laid in her resting place the wounds will start to heal, and I don't just mean the broken bones.'

'I didn't know it was as bad as that,' her father said. 'What do you recommend? Counselling?'

'Maybe. But I think Imogen has enough strength of character to come through this. Just as long as we are all there for her when she needs us. For myself, I'm prepared to take a back seat when the memory of it all becomes too much for her.

'You don't deserve this,' Brian said gruffly.

'Possibly,' Blair told him wryly, 'but, then, neither does she.'

There was an autumn nip in the air the following morning as they made their way to the small chapel in the grounds of the hospital, with Blair pushing Imogen in a wheelchair and Celia and Brian following on behind.

Back in the ward he'd watched in mute anguish as she'd placed a spray of tiny pink rosebuds on top of the small white coffin and now she was holding it on her knees.

He was dressed in a dark suit, white shirt and black tie, and when he'd arrived Imogen had thought in sudden despair that she wished all the ice inside her would melt.

Blair was everything she'd ever wanted. Kind, caring, strong, and so achingly attractive she couldn't believe that she was behaving the way she was.

She knew she was hurting him, treating him badly, but it was as if she was no longer responsible for her actions. Some kind of out-of-hand force was driving her towards self-punishment and Blair was getting the backlash.

It was worse because she was captive in the hospital through her injuries. If she hadn't been, she would have been long gone to somewhere where she could be alone to weep out her misery and get her life into perspective again.

As he'd tucked a rug around her legs he'd said, 'I shall sit at the back during the service. If you need me, you have only to call.'

She'd nodded mutely and he prayed again that once this was over things might change.

The hospital chaplain was waiting for them and when he'd taken the tiny coffin and placed it in front of the altar the service began.

It was reverent, and very moving, and Imogen was the only one not weeping. Blair wished she had been, but he surmised that she kept her tears for when she was alone.

From there they went to the cemetery for a short

burial service before the coffin was placed in what was called 'the baby circle', where babies like Joy were buried in the company of other infants.

It was a tranquil and beautiful place, and once the service was over they left Imogen to say her own private goodbye before making their way back to the hospital.

Her face was bleached as if her lifeblood had drained away in the last few hours, but she was still dry-eyed and in the grip of cold composure. But it cracked momentarily when her father announced on the way back that he was due to have a heart bypass in the very near future.

'I didn't want to mention it until today's ceremony was over,' he told her, and Blair, who was aware of what the cardiac consultant's report had said, was impressed by his consideration for his daughter.

'You should have told me!' she protested weakly. 'I've been very selfish of late, thinking only of myself.' She turned to Blair, making him feel once more that he couldn't do right for doing wrong, 'Why didn't *you* tell me?'

'I didn't think it my place,' he said levelly. 'Your father needed to tell you himself.'

When they arrived back at the hospital a nurse was hovering to get Imogen settled back into the ward. Seeing her exhaustion, Blair didn't linger as he knew she wanted him to go anyway.

When her father and Celia followed him shortly afterwards Imogen breathed a sigh of relief. The ordeal that she'd been dreading was over. Joy Gabriella Rossiter had been laid to rest with other babies who had never seen the light of day, and maybe now she could start making plans.

Sadly, at this moment in time they weren't going to include Blair as it was still there, the confusion of mind and purpose that she'd experienced ever since losing her baby.

There was talk of her being discharged and she'd asked that when a date had been decided upon she would be told before anyone else. In her apartment was a half-papered nursery that she was going to have to face, and she didn't want any onlookers on that occasion.

Then there was her place at the practice, which from all accounts was being admirably filled by Andrew's friend. Did she want to go back?

What did it matter? she thought exhaustedly. What did anything matter? With the thought, the tears that she'd held back came, torrents of them, turning her pillow and the front of her nightdress into limp dampness.

For the rest of the day Blair put the sad little funeral to the back of his mind. He knew he had to or he would go insane. Never, ever for the rest of his life did he want to have to go through something like that again.

He'd decided that if there were going to be any new beginnings for Imogen and himself, the bedroom at her apartment would have to be stripped of its nursery paper. He couldn't let his beautiful girl come home to that. And so on his way home from the practice he stopped off and got to work.

It didn't take long. Once the walls were bare again he stashed away the paint pots, the remaining wallpaper and the rest of the things that Imogen had used so that the room looked as it had before. Then home for a quick bite and back to the hospital.

Imogen's red-rimmed eyes told him that the tears had been shed and wiped away, and relief swept over him. Bottling up grief did no one any good.

She smiled when she saw him and his heartbeat quickened. It was a grimace compared to her usual beam but it was something to hold onto.

'And so how does the world look tonight?' he asked gently.

He realised he'd been presuming too much when she said flatly, 'Just as grey and empty as before.'

'Even though, according to the night staff, you're having the casts taken off tomorrow? You'll soon be going home, Imogen. As soon as they say you're going to be discharged, ring me and I'll come and pick you up.'

'Yes, all right,' she agreed without any show of enthusiasm.

'Why don't I take you to my place for the first few weeks?' he suggested.

He wanted her with him more than anything else on earth, and it was one way of finding out how things stood between them.

The gargoyle smile was back. 'I'll have to think about it,' she said, and he had to be content with that.

When he'd gone she lay back against the pillows and thought it would serve her right if he did hitch up with Briony because she was treating him abominably.

Only a few weeks ago she would have jumped at the invitation to stay at his place, but now she had no intention of doing any such thing.

Everything had changed between them. She was free now. No longer the pregnant woman. Life would be so simple if she could go to him and tell him she still loved him, but she couldn't. It would be as if the cost of happiness was losing her child.

She hadn't told him but she already knew when she was being discharged and had made arrangements accordingly. Her father and Celia knew what she was going to do and approved of her plans up to a point, but when she'd sworn them to secrecy neither of them had been happy about what she was doing to Blair.

And she was sure that if her father had still been the man he'd been before her accident and before he'd discovered that he needed a heart bypass, he would have had a lot to say about her behaviour. But as it was, he'd briefly expressed his disapproval and had then let the matter drop.

All loose ends were now tied up. Her tiny daughter had been laid to rest. The relationship with her father, though still leaving a lot to be desired, was better than it had ever been, and once Blair found that she'd gone he would give up on her. Further than that she couldn't think.

CHAPTER TEN

WHEN Blair arrived at the hospital the following night he stopped in his tracks in the doorway of the small side ward where Imogen had been ever since the accident.

There was a new patient in the bed, eyeing him curiously from beneath the covers, and alarm gripped him, but only for a second. They would have contacted him if anything had happened to her, he reasoned. Which left an explanation for her disappearance. She'd been discharged.

With an apologetic smile for the woman in the bed he turned quickly and went to seek out the sister.

'Yes, Dr Rossiter has been discharged,' she told him in answer to his tight-lipped enquiry. 'I'm sorry that you weren't informed, but that was how she wanted it.'

'I see,' he said sombrely. 'And would you know where she's gone?'

'I have no specific details,' she said evenly. 'All I know is that she has moved into convalescent care. A private ambulance took her there this morning and any further treatment she requires, such as physiotherapy, will be carried out there.'

'Thank you, Sister,' he said with flat politeness.

'We did think it strange that she left in that way,' she went on, 'especially after the devotion you've shown her, but I suppose she had her reasons.'

'Yes, no doubt she had,' he remarked as he turned to go, and told himself silently that the staff probably thought he was some sort of pest, a stalking type that Imogen was glad to get away from.

Blair felt sick inside. Not a word of goodbye, not a hint of what she'd been planning. Yet he couldn't blame her. Nothing was making sense to her at the present time. She was suffering and was making it clear that she wanted it to be in private.

Did the Rossiters know about this? he wondered. He would soon find out. Pulling up at the side of the road, he rang her father's house.

Celia answered the phone and she sounded uncomfortable.

'Yes, we did know what Imogen was planning,' she said, 'and, Blair, neither Brian nor I think it is fair, what she's done to you. We told her so in no uncertain terms and, when she swore us to secrecy regarding her whereabouts, we were reluctant to agree. But the poor girl has been in such a dark mood ever since she lost the baby and we couldn't distress her further by refusing to do as she asked.'

'I don't want you to break your promise,' he told her. 'I have to respect Imogen's wishes. I was in love with her, still am, but I realise now that I've gone about it all the wrong way. When I found out that she was pregnant I backed off because it didn't seem right somehow. I was prepared to wait until the baby was born before telling her how I feel, even though I was aware that *she* wasn't prepared to deny *her* feelings until that time. And now I've blown it. Left it too late.

'She seems to think that my concern is merely because I'm sorry for her and she wants none of it. Lots of women suffer from depression when they've had a safe delivery and given birth to a healthy child, so what it must be like for Imogen none of us can possibly imagine. But taking all that into account, I do feel that she might at least have said goodbye.'

The room was delightful. Large, airy and tastefully furnished, it looked out onto luxuriant gardens and beyond them was the sea and the beach where she and Blair had picnicked in the summer darkness an eternity ago.

When she'd been checking through lists of convalescent homes, the details for this one had sprung up at her from the page and her father had said immediately, 'If that's where you want to go, I'll meet the cost. I'll do anything to get you back to health and strength again.'

As she'd hugged him gratefully, Imogen had thought that it was ironic that losing her baby had brought them together and separated her and Blair.

But her father had been offering her the chance to be alone, the opportunity to sort out her thoughts away from those she loved. Maybe one day the original Imogen Rossiter would appear, sadder, wiser but ready to start living again. If by that time Blair had found himself someone else then she would have to accept it.

When Blair explained to George that Imogen wouldn't be coming back, the elderly GP said, 'It suits me to stay on if you want me to, but I won't mind if you want to bring in a younger person.'

'I'm going to leave it for the time being,' Blair told him. 'I will have to take on a new partner in the near future, but for the moment I'm glad to have you here.'

He'd told the staff at the practice that he and Imogen had split up and that she'd left the district. There'd been no questions asked, but he knew they must have heard what had happened from Lauren who would have heard it from Simon.

He didn't care whether they knew or not, he'd thought grimly. He was going to have to get on with his life the best he could and file away the time spent with Imogen as a beautiful blip.

But it wasn't that easy. Every time he saw George in Imogen's consulting room he ached for him to be her. When he drove past her empty apartment he wanted to get out of the car, ring the doorbell and imagine that she was going to open the door.

When he was called to the police station the memories were there, too, and he sometimes wished that he could pull up sticks like she had.

As October stepped back to let in a mild November, the sun and sea air were fulfilling their promise. Imogen was beginning to feel well again, awakening each morning with a little more purpose in her than the day before.

She was booked into the convalescent home for a month and when that time was up she was going to have to decide where next. Her father and Celia had a villa in Spain and they'd suggested that she go there, but she wasn't sure.

It suited her to be in this place where she'd been with Blair. Her mind often went back to when she'd pleaded with him not to look when she'd stood before him in pregnant nakedness and instead he'd made her feel beautiful.

She wouldn't want him to look now either, she thought one day as she strolled along the deserted beach with the scars of the most disastrous day of her life still vivid across her midriff.

Yet her smile was tender. He'd loved her for what she was. Had made her feel precious and wanted. Why couldn't she have told him how much she was hurting instead of shutting him out?

Imogen had been at the convalescent home three weeks and physically she was feeling so much better she couldn't believe it, but her state of mind was another matter.

Where before she hadn't wanted to see Blair, now she was missing him. She was ready to take up the threads of normal life again, but was he going to feel the same? She doubted it.

Celia had told her how hurt he'd been when she'd disappeared without even a goodbye, and she didn't blame him. He'd been incredibly patient and caring after she'd lost the baby, and what had she done? Pushed him out of her life.

She could imagine what he would say if she turned up now and told him she was ready to take up where they'd left off, that she still loved him desperately. Yet the first move, if any, was up to her. Blair had done what he could to keep them together, and she'd been too desolate to respond.

The fact that she wasn't making any plans to continue hiding away from him was proof enough of what was in her heart, but had she got enough of her zest back to go to him?

A solution presented itself with a visit from her father and Celia. Brian had two things to tell his daughter. The first was that he was to have the heart bypass the following week. The second was that the trial of the man who'd killed the teenagers in the park was also due to take place at the same time.

'The prosecution will be calling Blair and you as

witnesses,' he told her. 'In your case because the fellow confessed to you that he'd killed the couple in the park, and also because he attacked you soon afterwards, which will bring an extra charge of attempted murder.

'Blair will need to be there because he was called out by the police when the first body was found, and he'll have to testify that he found the fellow trying to strangle you. If you're not up to it, I'll try to get them to postpone the trial,' he told her, but she shook her head.

'No, I'm fine. I really do feel so much better...and I want to see that man punished for what he did to those poor young people.'

'And you're ready to talk to Blair?' Celia probed gently.

'Yes, if he'll talk to me.'

'You must come and stay with us while the trial is on,' her father suggested, but Imogen shook her head.

'No. I'll go back to the apartment. I need to get used to living there again.'

She hadn't been back there since she'd lost the baby as Celia had packed a case for her when she'd decided to go to the convalescent home, and sooner or later she was going to have to face the empty, half-papered nursery.

When Blair heard that he would be required as a witness at the trial, the first thing he thought of was that so would Imogen. She would have to leave her hiding place, he thought sombrely. It would be the first time they'd seen each other in weeks, but she need have no fear.

He wasn't going to put any pressure on her in any shape or form. If she indicated that she wanted it to be a case of hello and goodbye, he would go along with it.

In any other circumstances he would have acted very differently, ready to fight for happiness for them both. But what Imogen had gone through made him feel that his hands were tied. It wasn't just a lovers' quarrel that was keeping them apart.

That was the sad thing. It wasn't a quarrel at all. It was a drifting-apart situation, like walking through fog. For the first time in his life he couldn't see the way ahead clearly. All he knew was that every day without her was an empty void.

The law courts were set back amongst neat gardens on one of the main streets of the city, and Imogen had gone straight there from her coastal hideaway.

She'd travelled by train as her car was still garaged at the apartment, and intended staying the night there before driving back to the coast the next day to say goodbye to the staff at the home and collect her things.

As it had sped along the tracks she'd been bracing herself for what was to come, and it hadn't been the trauma of the trial that had been uppermost in her mind.

It had been horrendous at the time, the finding of the two bodies and her own subsequent ordeal at the hands of the crazed killer, but since then she'd been through a worse ordeal, which had left her scarred physically and mentally.

Today when she saw Blair she would know just how much her wounds had healed, and every time she thought about this meeting that the fates and the justice system were about to bring about her mouth went dry.

She was early and as an watery sun slanted onto the gardens she sat down on a nearby seat for a moment of respite before joining those bustling in and out of the building.

When she looked up, Blair was walking towards her, dark-suited, immaculate, as he'd been on the day of her baby's funeral. In sudden panic she thought today would be another funeral. The funeral of her hopes. She wanted him. Needed him. Couldn't believe how she'd ever thought she could exist without him.

He looked older, had lost the calm relaxed look that had been so much a part of him before, but he was still the most wantable man she'd ever met.

She got to her feet and when he drew level he said evenly, 'Imogen. Hello. You're honouring us with a flying visit, I see.'

Lost for words, she nodded mutely.

'You're looking well,' he commented in the same level tone. 'Have all the medical problems sorted themselves out?'

She noticed he had no comment to make about her state of mind past and present and, having no wish to get involved in a heart-to-heart in such surroundings, she said distantly, 'Yes, thank you.'

'So you're up to giving evidence.'

'Yes, of course,' she affirmed in the same tone.

'Right. So shall we go in, then?' he suggested, and stepped back to allow her to precede him.

She was wearing the navy blazer and bright red skirt that she'd worn on the night they'd met, and he thought that the constraint between them on that occasion had been as nothing compared to what was happening now.

Imogen did look well. Her face had regained its smooth perfection, her dark mop its lustre. Her lithe slenderness was back, but where was her spirit? Gone forever?

*   *   *

The time spent in the courtroom was harrowing and brought back dreadful memories, but Blair had been involved in similar cases before in his role as police surgeon and so had Imogen, though obviously her involvement had been to a much lesser degree.

There was little doubt what the verdicts would be in view of the man's confession to her and his attack upon her, and when Imogen went into the witness box she was a different person to the polite stranger that Blair had met in the gardens outside.

Her confidence was back. Her ability to make a point and stick to it was evident. It was only where he was concerned that she didn't seem to know her own mind, he thought soberly.

At the end of the day they were told that they wouldn't be needed again, and still with the huge barrier of constraint between them they prepared to go their separate ways.

'Where are you off to next?' he asked casually as they hesitated outside the law courts.

'Spain,' she said on the spur of the moment. 'My dad has a villa there.'

'Sounds good,' he said, still in the tone of someone asking out of politeness, then adding with a glance at the clock on the tower above the law courts, 'I might just be in time to call in at the practice to see how the day has gone.' He raised a quizzical eyebrow. 'You remember that place, do you?'

Imogen swallowed hard.

'Yes. I remember. I've been remembering a lot of things lately that I thought I wanted to forget and realising...'

Her voice had trailed away and he said gravely,

'Yes. I'm sure you have. It's all part of the recovery process.'

He was willing Imogen to take that first step, because it had to come from her otherwise he would never know if she really did want him back in her life.

But when she made no move, just stood in front of him silently, he turned to go.

Her face had whitened and, taking hold of his arm, she begged, 'Don't go, Blair.'

He turned back to face her and in that moment all his frustration surfaced. 'I thought that was how you preferred it…my company in small doses. Very small, if I remember rightly.'

Her hand fell away. She was getting the message.

'I'm sorry,' she said bleakly. 'Just how much you'll never know. I don't blame you for feeling as you do.' Now it was her turn to want to break up the disastrous reunion. 'Goodbye, Blair. I hope that life treats you more fairly in the future.' And before he had the chance to see the tears that were choking her, she left.

Late surgery was over and all the staff had gone when he got back to the practice, but Blair had no inclination to go home.

He'd treated Imogen shamefully back there at the law courts, he thought as he slumped into the chair behind his desk. Taken his hurt out on her like an immature adolescent, when all the time he'd been aching to take her in his arms and kiss her quivering mouth until it smiled again.

It was the moment he'd been longing for yet he'd been like a tongue-tied dummy, and when he had found his voice he'd said the most hurtful thing he could think of. What an idiot!

If their meeting today had been by chance, he would have been so enchanted to be with her again he would have swept her off her feet and worried about the consequences afterwards.

But knowing that she would be there because she had no choice, he'd had time to think about it. Warn himself to play it cool. Not to rush her. Give her time. And he'd certainly done that. Until no longer able to contain himself he'd lashed out.

Did he *want* to have to exist on the occasional postcard from Spain? He leapt to his feet. No! He did not!

When he got home, Simon was there. It was his night off and he immediately asked, 'How did it go?'

'Catastrophic,' Blair told him absently.

'What?' his young brother exclaimed. 'Don't say they've let him off!'

That tuned him in.

'Oh, you mean the trial.'

'What else?'

'Imogen was there. We'd both been called as witnesses. That was what was catastrophic. The trial went as we'd expected.'

'But not the romance?'

'Er…no. She's talking about going to live in Spain.'

'And you are going to let her?' Simon hooted. 'You, bro, are not the man I thought you were if you do. What are you doing here? Why aren't you at her place, plighting your troth?'

Blair was smiling.

'I'm on my way. I just stopped off to collect something that's been lying in the drawer for quite some time.'

He rang Celia before he set off to ask if she knew

where Imogen had gone after the court case. Brian had been admitted to hospital during the afternoon for the preliminaries of the operation, and Blair thought that she might be staying at his place, but Celia had said that Imogen was spending the night at her apartment as she had to go back some time and the sooner the better.

So she would have seen what he'd done to the nursery, Blair thought as he pulled up in front of the apartment block only minutes later. What would Imogen have to say about that? he wondered.

He wasn't to know that after putting off the moment ever since arriving home, she was about to go into the nursery, but his ring on the doorbell brought her to a halt with her hand on the doorhandle of what would have been the baby's room.

When she saw him standing outside the colour drained from her face. Opening the door slowly, she stepped back to let him in.

Accepting her invitation to enter, he strode over the threshold and stood observing her silently, knowing that this was one of the most important moments of their lives.

'I was just about to venture into the nursery,' she said jerkily, as if anxious to break the silence.

'So you've not been in there yet.'

'Er...no.'

'Would you like us to go in together?'

She nodded with her head bent.

'Yes. I would. I was dreading facing it alone.'

He took her hand in his and held it tightly.

'Come along, then,' he said gravely.

When she saw what he'd done, her face crumpled. '*You* did this for me, didn't you? To save me pain.'

'You've not asked me why I'm here. Don't you want to know?' he questioned gently.

'Yes, of course I do.'

'I'm here because I love you. Always have since the moment we met. I gave up when I should have had patience, the patience to let you find your way back to me in your own time.

'Dare I hope that what you said to me outside the law courts means that you *have* found your way back? That we can start making plans of our own? That this time when I ask you to marry me you'll know that it's because I can't live without you?'

The sparkle, so long missing, had come back to Imogen's eyes while he'd been speaking. She had thrown off the mute mantle of despair. The woman beneath it had come back to him as she told him smilingly, 'Yes, Blair, of course I'll marry you. I've known all along that you loved me, when I was pregnant and when I wasn't. But I hurt so much after losing my baby that I couldn't think straight. I felt that the happiness I craved with you had somehow been responsible for the awful thing that happened to me, but once I'd given myself time to look deep down in my subconscious I accepted that it had been just a terrible accident.'

'I know.' he told her tenderly. 'You've had a dreadful time, but the future is before us. You won't ever be alone again.' Taking her in his arms, he said softly with his mouth against the dark gloss of her hair, 'Do you remember that we once went to choose a ring and you changed your mind about marrying me just as we were about to go into the shop?'

She nodded.

'And how I said that diamonds weren't right for you because they are cold and glittering? That emeralds or rubies were the jewels for you because they're warm and glowing like you?'

'Yes, I remember,' she said wryly. 'Though I haven't exactly been warm and glowing of late, have I?'

'Maybe not, but I still bought the ring all that time ago, so sure was I that one day you would wear it on your finger. Admittedly, of late I've had some doubts, but now they've all disappeared. So close your eyes, my darling.'

When she opened them a small circlet of emeralds lay on her palm.

'Oh, Blair,' she whispered. 'I do love you so.'

Later, much later, Blair said, 'There'll be another nursery one day, Imogen, that will hold the babies that we make. And as they grow older, we'll tell them about their small sister sleeping not far away.'

LIVE THE EMOTION

Modern Romance™
...seduction and
passion guaranteed

Tender Romance™
...love affairs that
last a lifetime

Medical Romance™
...medical drama
on the pulse

Historical Romance™
...rich, vivid and
passionate

Sensual Romance™
...sassy, sexy and
seductive

Blaze Romance™
...the temperature's
rising

27 new titles every month.

Live the emotion

MILLS & BOON®

MB3

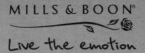

MILLS & BOON®

Live the emotion

Medical Romance™

STORMBOUND SURGEON *by Marion Lennox*

Joss Braden is bored. In fact he's out of Iluka as fast as
his sports car can take him! But the bridge is down –
there's no way on or off the headland. Suddenly Joss is
responsible for a whole town's health, with only Amy
Freye's nursing home as a makeshift hospital – and the
chemistry between Joss and Amy is incredible!

OUTBACK SURGEON *by Leah Martyn*

Gorgeous Nick Tonnelli isn't just a high-flying
surgeon, he's also a Sydney socialite. Outback GP
Abbey Jones is charmed but confused when he makes
his interest clear. The attraction between them is
overwhelming, but will the glamorous surgeon really
want a relationship with her?

THE DOCTOR'S ENGAGEMENT WISH
by Gill Sanderson

Erin Hunter had been the most beautiful girl at school
– and like all the boys Josh Harrison had been in love
with her. Now they have been reunited, while
working as GPs, and Josh finds his attraction to Erin as
strong as ever. But Erin isn't as carefree as he
remembers, and he is determined to discover what
has changed her...

On sale 4th July 2003

*Available at most branches of WH Smith, Tesco, Martins, Borders,
Eason, Sainsbury's and all good paperback bookshops.*

0603/03a

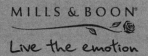

MILLS & BOON

Live the emotion

Medical Romance™

DR SOTIRIS'S WOMAN *by Margaret Barker*

Dr Francesca Metcalfe is the most gorgeous woman Dr Sotiris Popadopoulos has ever seen, and while they are working together on Ceres Island he hopes they will get to know each other better. But it seems that Francesca has chosen her career over having a family, and Sotiris has his young son who is need of a mother...

HER SPECIAL CHILD *by Kate Hardy*

One look at locum GP Tina Lawson and Dr Alex Bowen is smitten – surely she must feel the same? She certainly does – but she can't risk getting involved with Alex. Her son Josh needs all her love and attention. But Alex is determined to prove passion will last – and two is better than one when it comes to caring for such a special little boy.

EMERGENCY AT VALLEY HOSPITAL
by Joanna Neil

Mistaking consultant Jake Balfour for a patient is bad enough – and if only he weren't so attractive... When Carys's sister is injured Jake's support is unexpected – but ever since her troubled childhood Carys has sworn off men. Could Jake be the man to change her mind?

On sale 4th July 2003

Available at most branches of WH Smith, Tesco, Martins, Borders, Eason, Sainsbury's and all good paperback bookshops.

0603/03b

Medical Romance™

...catch the fever

We're on the lookout for fresh talent!

Think you have what it takes to write a novel?

Then this is your chance!

Can you:

✳ Create heroes and heroines who are dedicated, attractive, up-to-the-minute medical professionals who would move a mountain to save a life or resolve a medical case?

✳ Create highly contemporary medical communities and settings – city and country hospitals, GP practices, A&E Depts, Special Care Baby Units, IVF clinics, Emergency Response Units, midwifery, paediatrics, maternity, etc?

✳ Create fast-paced medical drama – think ER, Casualty, Holby City, Peak Practice, etc.

✳ Develop deeply emotional stories, ranging from the tender to the passionate, of medical professionals falling in love amidst the pulse-raising drama of their everyday lives?

If so, we want to hear from you!

Visit www.millsandboon.co.uk for editorial guidelines.

Submit the first three chapters and synopsis to:
Harlequin Mills & Boon Editorial Department,
Eton House, 18-24 Paradise Road,
Richmond, Surrey, TW9 1SR,
United Kingdom.   0203/WRITERS/MED

4 BOOKS
AND A SURPRISE GIFT!

We would like to take this opportunity to thank you for reading this Mills & Boon® book by offering you the chance to take FOUR more specially selected titles from the Medical Romance™ series absolutely FREE! We're also making this offer to introduce you to the benefits of the Reader Service™—

★ FREE home delivery ★ FREE gifts and competitions
★ FREE monthly Newsletter ★ Exclusive Reader Service discount
★ Books available before they're in the shops

Accepting these FREE books and gift places you under no obligation to buy; you may cancel at any time, even after receiving your free shipment. Simply complete your details below and return the entire page to the address below. *You don't even need a stamp!*

YES! Please send me 4 free Medical Romance books and a surprise gift. I understand that unless you hear from me, I will receive 6 superb new titles every month for just £2.60 each, postage and packing free. I am under no obligation to purchase any books and may cancel my subscription at any time. The free books and gift will be mine to keep in any case.

M3ZED

Ms/Mrs/Miss/Mr ....Initials ....
BLOCK CAPITALS PLEASE

Surname ....

Address ....

....

....Postcode ....

Send this whole page to:
UK: FREEPOST CN81, Croydon, CR9 3WZ
EIRE: PO Box 4546, Kilcock, County Kildare (stamp required)

Offer valid in UK and Eire only and not available to current Reader Service subscribers to this series. We reserve the right to refuse an application and applicants must be aged 18 years or over. Only one application per household. Terms and prices subject to change without notice. Offer expires 30th September 2003. As a result of this application, you may receive offers from Harlequin Mills & Boon and other carefully selected companies. If you would prefer not to share in this opportunity please write to The Data Manager at the address above.

Mills & Boon® is a registered trademark owned by Harlequin Mills & Boon Limited.
Medical Romance™ is being used as a trademark.